The Train
to Lo Wu

[s t o r i e s]

JESS ROW

dial press trade paperbacks

THE TRAIN TO LO WU
A Dial Press Trade Paperback Book

PUBLISHING HISTORY
Dial Press hardcover edition published February 2005
Dial Press Trade Paperback edition / February 2006

Published by The Dial Press
A Division of Random House, Inc.
New York, New York

The stories in this collection originally appeared, in different form, in the following publications and anthologies: "Revolutions" in *Green Mountains Review*, "The Secrets of Bats" and "The Train to Lo Wu" in *Ploughshares*, "The American Girl" in *Ontario Review*, "The Ferry" in *Threepenny Review*, "For You" in *Kyoto Journal*, and "Heaven Lake" in *Harvard Review*.

"The Secrets of Bats" appeared in *The Best American Short Stories 2001*, and *The Pushcart Prize XXVI: Best of the Small Presses*. "Heaven Lake" appeared in *The Best American Short Stories 2003*.

Book design by Virginia Norey

Library of Congress Catalog Card Number: 200456201
The Dial Press and Dial Press Trade Paperbacks are registered trademarks of Random House, Inc., and the colophon is a trademark of Random House, Inc.

ISBN-10: 0-385-33790-6
ISBN-13: 978-0-385-33790-8
Printed in the United States of America
Published simultaneously in Canada
www.dialpress.com

BVG   10 9 8 7 6 5 4 3 2

For Sonya

Praise for Jess Row's
THE TRAIN TO LO WU

"From New York to Hong Kong, Jess Row's stories take us to worlds that are both familiar and strange. It is rare to find the spirit and mind combined so deftly as in these stories. This is a magnificent collection."
—Charles Baxter

"In *The Train to Lo Wu* Jess Row has located the very heart of modern spirituality in this most commercial of cities. This is a debut that feels like a crowning achievement." —Edmund White

"[A]n intelligent and gifted young writer . . . [these stories] have an unusual subtlety and depth of insight." —*Baltimore Sun*

"Jess Row writes with elegance and freshness in prose that sounds a depth of feeling. These stories are poems in themselves, haunting in their clarity and sympathies. They achieve a kind of stillness that seems appropriate for their Chinese setting. I can hardly imagine a more forceful or memorable debut." —Jay Parini

"Over and over, these beautifully crafted stories drew me in with their quietly persuasive voices, their meditative detail, and their subtly heartrending plots. An auspicious debut from a talent set to endure."
—Peter Ho Davies

"In crystalline prose, Row animates intriguing characters and dramatizes subtle yet emblematic conflicts as he traces the vast cultural divides between America and Hong Kong. . . . He neatly and devastatingly contrasts dueling visions of faith, art, love, and freedom." —*Booklist*

"Row's poetic sensibility lends both depth and economy to each of the stories. . . . Elegant and original, mysterious and down-to-earth, these seven tales make for an auspicious, entertaining debut." —*Elle*

"In sharp, lucid prose, Row molds a landscape of human error and uncertainty, territory well-aligned with eerie topography of his space-age city." —*Publishers Weekly*

"An impressive debut from an admirably protean storyteller . . . Row's characters are a mixed bunch, but all are effortlessly convincing, and he handles gritty suspense quite as well as he does the problems of lovers. This Whiting Award–winning author has a very bright future."
—*Kirkus Reviews*

"Row's stories are subtle . . . and fascinating." —*Entertainment Weekly*

"The stories operate as intuitive, emotional, and, in some cases, romantic responses to one of the most unusual places on earth.... *The Train to Lo Wu* does something great: it opens our eyes to things, inside and out."
—*Believer*

"In these seven quiet, deftly drawn stories, characters crisscross various demarcations of politics, history, race, and religion, but, agonizingly, they never seem able to locate one another, let alone themselves."
—*Ploughshares*

"*The Train to Lo Wu* ... puts Row into a league above the many Western authors trying to capture the spirit of a culture that is not their own."
—*South China Morning Post*

"*The Train to Lo Wu* gives, with admirable breadth and depth, a believable and fluidly portrayed assortment of people, Western and Chinese, who are finding their ways in [Hong Kong].... Row is a clever and subtle writer; like real people, his characters surprise, annoy, and demand empathy from the reader." —*Shanghai City Weekend*

"Many writers have managed to describe Hong Kong, but few have as deft a touch with the Hong Kong people, real people.... Read these stories, re-read them, and then remember. You will be richer for it."
—*Asian Review of Books*

"These seven stories about Hong Kong people by a young American writer are not only subtle, skillful, and above all exceptionally thoughtful: they could well be the finest fiction ever to have appeared in English about the city. It's no exaggeration to say that *The Train to Lo Wu* is comparable in many ways with James Joyce's *Dubliners*." —*Taipei Times*

"The stories in *The Train to Lo Wu* ... are sensitive in exactly the right way. In a brave new transnational world they explore the intersection of loneliness and responsibility, where human contact may have to be fleeting in order to be genuine. Futuristic yet leading to a sense of lasting knowledge, these stories make a wonderful collection."
—Kate Wheeler, author of *Not Where I Started From* and *When Mountains Walked*

"These are not outsider's tales, taking their pleasure by making fun of a strange and foreign culture. This is a book about insiders of all kinds, smothered in their own heads, searching for a way out. It's an impressive debut collection, one that establishes Row as a promising young voice, with a voice spare and penetrating and, it must be said, entertaining."
—*New Haven Advocate*

Contents

You take delight not in a city's seven or seventy wonders,
but in the answer it gives to a question of yours.
Or the question it asks you, forcing you to answer...

—Italo Calvino, *Invisible Cities*

The Secrets
of Bats

Alice Leung has discovered the secrets of bats: how they see without seeing, how they own darkness, as we own light. She walks the halls with a black headband across her eyes, keening a high C—*cheat cheat cheat cheat cheat cheat*—never once veering off course, as if drawn by an invisible thread. Echolocation, she tells me; it's not as difficult as you might think. Now she sees a light around objects when she looks at them, like halos on her retinas from staring at the sun. In her journal she writes, *I had a dream that was all in blackness. Tell me how to describe.*

It is January: my fifth month in Hong Kong.

In the margin I write, *I wish I knew.*

After six, when the custodians leave, the school becomes a perfect acoustic chamber; she wanders from the basement laboratories to the basketball courts like a trapped bird looking for a window. She finds my door completely blind, she says, not counting flights or paces. Twisting her head from side to side like

3

Stevie Wonder, she announces her progress: another room mapped, a door, a desk, a globe, detected and identified by its aura.

You'll hurt yourself, I tell her. I've had nightmares: her foot missing the edge of a step, the dry crack of a leg breaking. Try it without the blindfold, I say. That way you can check yourself.

Her mouth wrinkles. This not important, she says. This only practice.

Practice for what, I want to ask. All the more reason you have to be careful.

You keep saying, she says, grabbing a piece of chalk. E-x-p-e-r-i-m-e-n-t, she writes on the blackboard, digging it in until it squeals.

That's right. Sometimes experiments fail.

Sometimes, she repeats. She eyes me suspiciously, as if I invented the word.

Go home, I tell her. She turns her pager off and leaves it in her locker; sometimes police appear at the school gate, shouting her name. Somebody, it seems, wants her back.

In the doorway she whirls, flipping her hair out of her eyes. Ten days more, she says. You listen. Maybe then you see why.

The name of the school is Po Sing Uk: a five-story concrete block, cracked and eroded by dirty rain, shoulder-to-shoulder with the tenements and garment factories of Cheung Sha Wan. No air-conditioning and no heat; in September I shouted to be heard over a giant fan, and now, in January, I teach in a winter jacket. When it rains, mildew spiderwebs across the ceiling of my classroom. Schoolgirls in white jumpers crowd into the room forty at a time, falling asleep over their textbooks, making furtive calls on mobile phones, scribbling notes to each other on pink Hello Kitty paper. If I call on one who hasn't raised her hand, she folds her arms across her chest and stares at the floor, and the room falls silent, as if by a secret signal. There is nothing more terrifying, I've found, than the echo of your own voice: *who are you?* It answers: *what are you doing here?*

I've come to see my life as a radiating circle of improbabilities that grow from each other, like ripples in water around a dropped stone. That I became a high school English teacher, that I work in another country, that I live in Hong Kong. That a city can be a mirage, hovering above the ground: skyscrapers built on mountainsides, islands swallowed in fog for days. That a language can have no tenses or articles, with seven different ways of saying the same syllable. That my best student stares at the blackboard only when I erase it.

She stayed behind on the first day of class: a tall girl with a narrow face, pinched around the mouth, her cheeks pitted with acne scars. Like most of my sixteen-year-olds she looked twelve, in a baggy uniform that hung to her knees like a sack. The others streamed past her without looking up, as if she were a boulder in the current; she stared down at my desk with a fierce vacancy, as if looking itself was an act of will.

How do you think about bats?

Bats?

She joined her hands at the wrist and fluttered them at me.

People are afraid of them, I said. I think they're very interesting.

Why? she said. Why very interesting?

Because they live in the dark, I said. We think of them as be-ing blind, but they aren't blind. They have a way of seeing, with sound waves—just like we see with light.

Yes, she said. I know this. Her body swayed slightly, in an imaginary breeze.

Are you interested in bats?

I am interest, she said. I want to know how— She made a face I'd already come to recognize: *I know how to say it in Chinese*—when one bat sees the other. The feeling.

You mean how one bat recognizes another?

Yes—recognize.

That's a good idea, I said. You can keep a journal about what you find. Write something in it every day.

She nodded vehemently, as if she'd already thought of that.

There are books on bat behavior that will tell you—

Not in books. She covered her eyes with one hand and walked forward until her hip brushed the side of my desk, then turned away, at a right angle. Like this, she said. There is a sound. I want to find the sound.

18 September
First hit tuning fork. Sing one octave higher: A B C. This
is best way.
Drink water or lips get dry.
I must have eyes totally closed. No light!!! So some kind
of black—like cloth—is good.
Start singing. First to the closest wall—sing and listen.
Practice ten times, 20 times. IMPORTANT: can not
move until I HEAR the wall. Take step back, one

time, two time. Listen again. I have to hear
DIFFERENCE first, then move.
Then take turn, ninety degrees left.
Then turn, one hundred eighty degrees left. Feel position
with feet. Feet very important—they are wings!!!

I don't know what this is, I told her the next day, opening the journal and pushing it across the desk. Can you help me?

I tell you already, she said. She hunched her shoulders so that her head seemed to rest on them, spreading her elbows to either side. It is like a test.

A test?

In the courtyard rain crackled against the asphalt; a warm wind lifted scraps of paper from the desk, somersaulting them through the air.

The sound, she said impatiently. I told you this.

I covered my mouth to hide a smile.

Alice, I said, humans can't do that. It isn't a learned behavior. It's something you study.

She pushed up the cover of the composition book and let it fall.

I think I can help you, I said. Can you tell me why you want to write this?

Why I want? She stared at me wide-eyed.

Why do you want to do this? What is the test for?

Her eyes lifted from my face to the blackboard behind me, moved to the right, then the left, as if measuring the dimensions of the room.

Why you want come to Hong Kong?

Many reasons, I said. After college I wanted to go to another country, and there was a special fellowship available here. And maybe someday I will be a teacher.

You are teacher.

I'm just learning, I said. I am trying to be one.

Then why you have to leave America?

I didn't, I said. The two things— I took off my glasses and rubbed my eyes. All at once I was exhausted; the effort seemed useless, a pointless evasion. When I looked up she was nodding slowly, as if I'd just said something profound.

I think I will find the reason for being here only after some time, I said. Do you know what I mean? There could be a purpose I don't know about.

So you don't know for good. Not sure.

You could say that.

Hai yat yeung, she said. This same. Maybe if you read you can tell me why.

This is what's so strange about her, I thought, studying her red-rimmed eyes, the tiny veins standing out like wires on a circuit-board. She doesn't look down. *I am fascinated by her,* I thought. *Is that fair?*

You're different from the others, I said. You're not afraid of me. Why is that?

Maybe I have other things be afraid of.

At first the fifth-floor bathroom was her echo chamber; she sat in one corner, on a stool taken from the physics room, and placed an object directly opposite her: a basketball, a glass, a feather. Sound waves triangulate, she told me, corners are best. Passing by, at the end of the day, I stopped, closing my eyes, and listened for the difference. She sang without stopping for five minutes, hardly taking a breath: almost a mechanical sound, as if someone had forgotten their mobile phone. Other teachers walked by in groups, talking loudly. If they noticed me, or the sound, I was never aware of it, but always, instinctively, I looked at my watch and followed them down the stairs. As if I too had to rush home to cook for hungry children, or boil medicine for my mother-in-law. I never stayed long enough to see if anything changed.

Document everything, I told her, and she did; now I have two binders of entries, forty-one in all. *Hallway. Chair. Notebook.* As if we were scientists writing a grant proposal, as if there were something actual to show at the end of it.

I don't keep a journal, or take photographs, and my letters home are factual and sparse. No one in Larchmont would believe me—not even my parents—if I told them the truth. *It sounds like quite an experience you're having! Don't get run over by a rickshaw.* And yet if I died tomorrow—why should I ever think this way?—these binders would be the record of my days. These and Alice herself, who looks out her window and with her eyes closed sees ships passing in the harbor, men walking silently in the streets.

26 January
Sound of lightbulb—low like bees hum. So hard to listen!

A week ago I dreamed of bodies breaking apart, arms and legs and torsos, fragments of bone, bits of tissue. I woke up flailing in the sheets, and remembered her immediately; there was too long a moment before I believed I was awake. *It has to stop,* I thought. *You have to say something.* Though I know I can't.

Perhaps there was a time when I might have told her, *this is ridiculous,* or, *You're sixteen, find some friends. What will people think?* But this is Hong Kong, of course, and I have no friends, no basis to judge. I leave the door open, always, and no one ever comes to check; we walk out through the gates together, late in the afternoon, past the watchman sleeping in his chair. For me she has a kind of professional courtesy, ignoring my whiteness politely, as if I had horns growing from my head. And she returns, at the end of each day, as a bat flies back to its cave at daybreak. All I have is time; who am I to pack my briefcase and turn away?

There was only once when I slipped up.

Pretend I've forgotten, I told her, one Monday in early October. The journal was open in front of us, the pages covered in red; she squinted down at it, as if instead of corrections I'd written hiero-glyphics. *I'm an English teacher,* I thought, *this is what I'm here for.* We should start again at the beginning, I said. Tell me what it is that you want to do here. You don't have to tell me about the project—just about the writing. Who are you writing these for? Who do you want to read them?

She stretched, catlike, curling her fingers like claws.

Because I don't think I understand, I said. I think you might want to find another teacher to help you. There could be some-thing you have in mind in Chinese that doesn't come across.

Not in Chinese, she said, as if I should have known that al-ready. In Chinese cannot say like this.

But it isn't really English either.

I know this. It is like both.

I can't teach that way, I said. You have to learn the rules before you can—

You are not teaching me.

Then what's the point?

She strode across the room to the window and leaned out, placing her hands on the sill and bending at the waist. Come here, she said; look. I stood up and walked over to her. She ducked her head down, like a gymnast on a bar, and tilted forward, her feet lifting off the floor.

Alice!

I grabbed her shoulder and jerked her upright. She stumbled, falling back; I caught her wrist and she pulled it away, steadying herself. We stood there a moment staring at each other, breathing in short huffs that echoed in the hallway.

Maybe I hear something and forget, she said. You catch me then. OK?

28 January
It is like photo negative, all the colors are the opposite.
Black sky, white trees, this way. But they are still
shapes—I can see them.

I read standing at the window, in a last sliver of sunlight. Alice stands on my desk, already well in shadow, turning around slowly as if trying to dizzy herself for a party game. Her winter uniform cardigan is three sizes too large; unbuttoned, it falls behind her like a cape.

This is beautiful.

Quiet, she hisses, eyebrows bunched together above her head-band. One second. There—there.

What is it?

A man on the stairs.

I go out into the hallway and stand at the top of the stairwell, listening. Five floors below, very faintly, I hear sandals skidding on the concrete, keys jangling on the janitor's ring.

You heard him open the gate, I say. That's cheating.

She shakes her head. I hear heartbeat.

The next Monday Principal Ho comes to see me during the lunch hour. He stands at the opposite end of the classroom, as always: a tall, slightly chubby man, in a tailored shirt, gold-rimmed glasses, and Italian shoes, who blinks as he reads the ESL posters I've tacked up on the wall. When he asks how my classes are, and I tell him that the girls are unmotivated, disengaged, he nods quickly, as if to save me the embarrassment. How lucky he was, he tells me, to go to boarding school in Australia, and then pronounces it with a flattened A, *Australhia,* so I have to laugh.

Principal Ho, I ask, do you know Alice Leung?

He turns his head toward me and blinks more rapidly. Leung Ka Yee, he says. Of course. You have problem with her?

No sir. I need something to hold; my hands dart across the desk behind me and find my red marking pen.

How does she perform?

She's very gifted. One of the best students in the class. Very creative.

He nods, scratches his nose, and turns away.

She likes to work alone, I say. The other girls don't pay much attention to her. I don't think she has many friends.

It is very difficult for her, he says slowly, measuring every word. Her mother is—her mother was a suicide.

In the courtyard, five stories down, someone drops a basketball and lets it bounce against the pavement; little *pings* that trill and fade into the infinite.

At Wo Che estate, Ho says. He makes a little gliding motion with his hand. Nowadays this is not so uncommon in Hong Kong. But still there are superstitions.

What kind of superstitions?

He frowns and shakes his head. Difficult to say in English. Maybe just that she is unlucky girl. Chinese people, you understand—some are still afraid of ghosts.

She isn't a ghost.

He gives a high-pitched, nervous laugh. No, no, he says. Not her. He puts his hands into his pockets, searching for something. Difficult to explain. I'm sorry.

Is there someone she can talk to?

He raises his eyebrows. *A counselor*, I am about to say, and explain what it means, when my hand relaxes, and I realize I have been crushing the pen in my palm. For a moment I am waterskiing again at Lake Patchogue: releasing the handle, settling against the surface, enfolded in water. When I look up Ho glances at his watch.

If you have any problem you can talk to me.

It's nothing, I say. Just curious, that's all.

She wears the headband all the time now, I've noticed: pulling it over her eyes whenever possible, in the halls between classes, in the courtyard at lunchtime, sitting by herself. No one shoves her or calls her names; she passes through the crowds unseen. If possible, I think, she's grown thinner, her skin translucent, blue veins showing at the wrists. Occasionally I notice the other teachers shadowing her, frowning, their arms crossed, but if our eyes meet they stare through me, disinterested, and look away.

I have to talk to you about something.

She is sitting in a desk at the far end of the room, reading her chemistry textbook, drinking from a can of soymilk with a straw. When the straw gurgles she bangs the can down, and we sit silently, the sound reverberating in the hallway.

I give you another journal soon. Two more days.

Not about that.

She doesn't move: fixed, alert, waiting. I walk down the aisle toward her and sit down two desks away. Her eyes follow me, growing rounder; her cheeks puff out, as if she's holding her breath.

Alice, I say, can you tell me about your mother?

Her hands drop onto the desk, and the can clatters to the floor, white drops spinning in the air.

Mother? Who tell you I have mother?

It's all right—

I reach over to touch one hand and she snatches it back.

Who tell you?

It doesn't matter. You don't have to be angry.

You big mistake, she says, wild-eyed, taking long swallows of air and spitting them out. Why you have to come here and mess everything?

I don't understand, I say. Alice, what did I do?

I trust you, she says, and pushes the heel of one palm against her cheek. I write and you read. I *trust* you.

What did you expect, I ask, my jaw trembling. Did you think I would never know?

Believe me. She looks at me pleadingly. Believe *me*.

Two days later she leaves her notebook on my desk, with a note stuck to the top. *You keep.*

1 February
Now I am finished
It is out there I hear it

I call out to her after class, and she hesitates in the doorway for a moment before turning, pushing her back against the wall.

Tell me what it was like, I say. Was it a voice? Did you hear someone speaking?

Of course no voice. Not so close to me. It was a feeling.

How did it feel?

She reaches up and slides the headband over her eyes.

It is all finish, she says. You not worry about me anymore.

Too late, I say. I stand up from my chair and take a tentative step toward her, weak-kneed, as if it were a staircase in the dark. You chose me, I say. Remember?

Go back to America. Then you forget all about this crazy girl.

This is my life too. Did you forget about that?

She raises her head and listens, and I know what she hears: a stranger's voice, as surely as if someone else had entered the room. She nods. *Who do you see,* I wonder, *what will he do next?* I reach out blindly, and my hand misses the door; on the second try I close it.

I choose this, I say. I'm waiting. Tell me.

Her body sinks into a crouch; she hugs her knees and tilts her head back.

Warm. It was warm. It was—it was a body.

But not close to you?

Not close. Only little feeling, then no more.

Did it know you were there?

No.

How can you be sure?

When I look up to repeat the question, shiny tracks of tears have run out from under the blindfold.

I am sorry, she says. She reaches into her backpack and splits open a packet of tissues without looking down, her fingers nimble, almost autonomous. You are my good friend, she says, and takes off the blindfold, turning her face to the side and dabbing her eyes. Thank you for help me.

It isn't over, I say. How can it be over?

Like you say. Sometimes experiment fails.

No, I say, too loudly, startling us both. It isn't that easy. You have to prove it to me.

Prove it you?

Show me how it works. I take a deep breath. I believe you. Will you catch me?

Her eyes widen, and she does not look away; the world swims around her irises. Tonight, she says, and writes something on a slip of paper, not looking down. I see you then.

In a week it will be the New Year: all along the streets the shop fronts are hung with firecrackers, red-and-gold character scrolls, pictures of grinning cats and the twin cherubs of good luck. Mothers lead little boys dressed in red silk pajamas, girls with New Year's pigtails. The old woman sitting next to me on the bus is busily stuffing twenty-dollar bills into red *lai see* packets: lucky money for the year to come. When I turn my head from the window, she holds one out to me, and I take it with both hands, automatically, bowing my head. This will make you rich, she says to me in Cantonese. And lots of children.

Thank you, I say. The same to you.

She laughs. Already happened. Jade bangles clink together as she holds up her fingers. Thirteen grandchildren! she says. Six boys. All fat and good-looking. You should say live long life to me.

I'm sorry. My Chinese is terrible.

No, it's very good, she says. You were born in Hong Kong?

Outside night is just falling, and Nathan Road has become a canyon of light: blazing neon signs, brilliant shop windows, decorations blinking across the fronts of half-finished tower blocks. I stare at myself a moment in the reflection, three red characters passing across my forehead, and look away. No, I say. In America. I've lived here only since August.

Ah. Then what is America like?

Forgive me, aunt, I say. I forget.

Prosperous Garden no. 4. Tung Kun Street. Yau Ma Tei.

A scribble of Chinese characters.

Show this to doorman he let you in

The building is on the far edge of Kowloon, next to the reclamation; a low concrete barrier separates it from an elevated highway that thunders continuously as cars pass. Four identical towers around a courtyard, long poles draped with laundry jutting from every window, like spears hung with old rotted flags.

Gong hei fat choi, I say to the doorman through the gate, and he smiles with crooked teeth, but when I pass the note to him all expression leaves his face; he presses the buzzer and turns away quickly. Twenty-three A-ah, he calls out to the opposite wall. You understand?

Thank you.

When I step out into the hallway I breathe in boiled chicken, oyster sauce, frying oil, the acrid steam of medicine, dried fish, Dettol. Two young boys are crouched at the far end, sending a radio-controlled car zipping past me; someone is arguing loudly over the telephone; a stereo plays loud Canto-pop from a balcony somewhere below. All the apartment doors are open, I notice as I walk by, and only the heavy sliding gates in front of them are closed. Like a honeycomb, I can't help thinking, or an ant farm. But when I reach 23A the door behind the gate is shut, and no sound comes from behind it. The bell sounds several times before the locks begin to snap open.

You are early, Alice says, rubbing her eyes, as if she's been sleeping. Behind her the apartment is dark; there is only a faint blue glow, as if from a TV screen.

I'm sorry. You didn't say when to come. I look at my watch: eight thirty. I can come back, I say, another time, maybe another night—

She shakes her head and opens the gate.

When she turns on the light I draw a deep breath, involuntarily, and hide it with a cough. The walls are covered with stacks of yellowed paper, file boxes, brown envelopes, and ragged books; on opposite sides of the room are two desks, each holding a computer with a flickering screen. I peer at the one closest to the door. At the top of the screen there is a rotating globe, and below it, a ribbon of letters and numbers, always changing. The other, I see, is just the same: a head staring at its twin.

Come, Alice says. She had disappeared for a moment and reemerged dressed in a long dress, silver running shoes, a hooded sweatshirt.

Are these computers yours?

No. My father's.

Why does he need two? They're just the same.

Nysee, she says, impatiently, pointing. Footsie. New York Stock Exchange. London Stock Exchange.

Sau Yee, a hoarse voice calls from another room. Who is it?

It's my English teacher, she says loudly. Giving me a home-work assignment.

Gwailo a?

Yes, she says. The white one.

Then call a taxi for him. He appears in the kitchen doorway: a stooped old man, perhaps five feet tall, in a dirty white T-shirt, shorts, and sandals. His face is covered with liver spots; his eyes shrunken into their sockets. I sorry-ah, he says to me. No speakee English.

It's all right, I say. There is a numbness growing behind my eyes: I want to speak to him, but the words are all jumbled, and Alice's eyes burning on my neck. Good-bye, I say, take care.

See later-ah.

Alice pulls the hood over her head and opens the door.

She leads me to the top of a dark stairwell, in front of a rusting door with light pouring through its cracks. *Tin paang,* she says, reading the characters stenciled on it in white. Roof. She hands me a black headband, identical to her own.

Hold on, I say, gripping the railing with both hands. The numbness behind my eyes is still there, and I feel my knees growing weak, as if there were no building below me, only a framework of girders and air. Can you answer me a question?

Maybe one.

Has he always been like that?

What like?

With the computers, I say. Does he do that all the time?

Always. Never turn them off.

In the darkness I can barely see her face: only the eyes, shining, daring me to speak. *If I were in your place,* I say to myself, and the phrase dissolves, weightless.

Listen, I say. I'm not sure I'm ready.

She laughs. When you be sure?

Her fingers fall across my face, and I feel the elastic brushing over my hair, and then the world is black. I open my eyes and close them: no difference.

We just go for a little walk, she says. You don't worry. Only listen.

I never realized, before, the weight of the air: at every step I feel the great mass of it pressing against my face, saddled on my shoulders. I am breathing huge quantities, as if my lungs were a giant recirculation machine, and sweat is running down from my forehead and soaking the edge of the headband. Alice takes normal-size steps, and grips my hand fiercely, so I can't let go. Don't be afraid, she shouts. We still in the middle. Not near the edge.

What am I supposed to do?

Nothing, she says. Only wait. Maybe you see something.

I stare, fiercely, into blackness, into my own eyelids. There is the afterglow of the hallway light, and the computer screens, very faint; or am I imagining it? What is there on a roof, I wonder, and try to picture it: television antennas, heating ducts, clotheslines. Are there guardrails? I've never seen any on a Hong Kong building. She turns, and I brush something metal with my hand. Do you know where you're going? I shout.

Here, she says, and stops. I stumble into her, and she catches my shoulder. Careful, she says. We wait here.

Wait for what?

Just listen, she says. I tell to you. Look to left side: there's a big building there. Very tall white building, higher than us. Small windows.

All right. I can see that.

Right side is highway. Very bright. Many cars and trucks passing.

If I strain to listen I can hear a steady whooshing sound, and then the high whine of a motorcycle, like a mosquito passing my ear. OK, I say. Got that.

In the middle is very dark. Small buildings. Only few lights on.

Not enough, I say.

One window close to us, she says. Two little children there. You see them?

No.

Lift your arm, she says, and I do. Put your hand up. See? They wave to you.

My god, I say. How do you do that?

She squeezes my hand.

You promise me something.

Of course. What is it?

You don't take it off, she says. No matter nothing. You promise me?

I do. I promise.

She lets go of my hand, and I hear running steps, soles skidding on concrete.

Alice! I shout, rooted to the spot; I crouch down, and balance myself with my hands. Alice! You don't—

Mama, she screams, ten feet away, and the sound carries, echoes; I can see it slanting with the wind, bright as daylight, as if a roman candle had exploded in my face. *Mama mama mama mama mama mama mama,* she sings, and I am crawling toward her on hands and knees, feeling in front of me for the edge.

She is there, Alice shouts. You see? She is in the air.

I see her. Stay where you are.

You watch, she says. I follow her.

She doesn't want you, I shout. She doesn't want you there. Let her go.

There is a long silence, and I stay where I am, the damp concrete soaking through to my knees. My ears are ringing, and the numbness has blossomed through my head; I feel faintly seasick.

Alice?

You can stand up, she says in a small voice, and I do.

You are shaking, she says. She puts her arms around me from behind and clasps my chest, pressing her head against my back. I thank you, she says.

She unties the headband.

6 February
Man waves white hands at black sky
He says arent you happy be alive
arent you
He kneels and kisses floor

The American Girl

A ll night, half-asleep, the boy feels the train around him as it moves.

He is pushed tight against the wall of the compartment: his older sister sleeps beside him, next to the rail, curled around her doll. When the train pulls into a station he feels its braking as a series of taps against his body, and then a long, sustained push, as if hands had reached out to restrain him. Once they have stopped, the folding stairs clatter against the platform and the trainman's boots thump along the walkway. Sanjiang, he shouts. Names the boy has never heard and never will again. Muffled voices, a few stumbling footsteps. Cigarette smoke.

Is this it? he wonders. Is this the end?

Far down the tracks he hears the first whistle, and then a deep vibration runs through the couplings, a tremor, as if the earth has moved. The train groans, nudging his shoulder as it begins to roll. He releases a deep breath. As they pull away from the platform, the lights of the station flicker against his eyelids and go out.

Standing on the sidewalk, unfolding his cane, Chen sniffs the morning air. There is a certain dampness in it, a tang of soil and new leaves; it blows across his face like an exhalation. The city breathes, he thinks. Spring. He turns his face to the left, north, where he has been told green hills rise above Kowloon. He nods, slaps his cane against the sidewalk, and begins walking.

From the door of his building to Lao Jiang's apothecary takes two hundred and thirty-four steps.

Passing Grandma Leung's noodle shop, he lifts his head: the smell of fishballs, pig's blood, fresh hot soymilk. Eh, Blind Chow! she calls from her window. His name is not Chow. But why correct her? He lifts a finger in the direction of the sound.

At the corner he turns left. A girl scolds her boyfriend for missing a date.

Dim gaai m'hoh yih da din wah—

A bus stops at the corner: whoosh of air brakes.

Newspapers crumple underfoot outside the Jockey Club parlor.

Old man, he tells himself, pay attention. No daydreaming.

A whiff of bitter herbs: he turns sharply and ducks into the shop, folding his cane as he does so.

He and Lao Jiang have worked together so long they hardly need to speak. In the rare event of a new patient Jiang will come into the massage room and tap on Chen's knee, or ankle, and grunt a few words in Shanghainese. Even that is usually unnecessary, for Chen's fingers know the source of tension immediately, as soon as they touch the skin: they have long since stopped doing his bidding.

Cantonese opera plays on a tinny transistor in the back room. Some of his old women patients are so talkative they cannot stop themselves, even in his strange company, and so he has known them for years, their agonies and triumphs: thousands won at mah-jongg, sons made managing directors, grandchildren moved to Canada and Australia and America. His mind wanders and comes to rest.

Each day, it seems to him, it becomes harder to resist, as if a trapdoor has been pushed back in the floor of his mind, and light floods in. At first only details come into focus: the ragged edge of a blanket, rust flaking from an iron frame. Faces appear, their lips moving silently, then voices.

I have to go to the bathroom, the boy announces.

At the end of the car, his father mumbles from the bunk below.

He wriggles out of the blankets and scrambles down the rungs to the floor. The cold blazes against his skin. Pulling his shoes on, he gazes in wonder at the etchings of frost on the window glass.

North, he thinks. We are headed north.

He runs, soles thumping along the walkway.

Why, he wonders. Why, why? What good does it do anyone?

Mr. Chen?

He lifts his face toward the sound.

Mr. Chen? It's Jill Marcus.

Sit down, he says, drink some tea. With you in a minute.

❖

Her first name is unpronounceable to him: the nearest he can get is *jir*, no matter how hard he tries. So he calls her *Xiao Ma*, with a rising tone: Little Horse. His private joke. She is a full head taller than he is; when she comes near he feels himself speaking to her shoulder. Long hair, unbraided, that moves the air around her when she turns. Blue eyes, so she says. A smell of lavender enters the shop with her and lingers for hours after she leaves.

Her skirt rustles as she crosses in front of the doorway.

I'm sorry I'm late.

Yes. I watch the clock for you.

She giggles, like a girl, and he hears the pages of the newspaper crackling as she opens it.

He doesn't remember how long she's been coming to the shop, having lost the habit of counting months and days. Since the previous summer, perhaps. Twice a week she sits in a chair to the side of the room, reading aloud to him while he gives massages and touches pressure points. The old women are respectfully silent, uncomprehending; even when she reads from the Chinese newspapers, her Beijing accent is impossible for them to follow. He prefers the gaps and slurs of her English, her flat, nasal way of making even familiar words strange. The name of her home place is *a ka la hou ma*, Oklahoma; he savors the sound, like the taste of a strange fruit.

He has forgotten how she found him, whether it was through Community Chest or Services for the Blind, but it hardly matters. Nor does he care what she chooses to read: about China, anything happening in China—a fire in an oil refinery in Liaoning, a chess competition won by twins in Wuhan. She is a little bit obsessed, he thinks, even for a *yanjiu sheng*, a graduate student. But the important thing is that she comes like clockwork, like a wake-up call.

Today it is an article about village elections in Shandong province, long and full of difficult English words. He waits, half-listening, for a gap—a page turning, a sip of water—and changes the subject.

How your research is going?

Almost finished, she says. Soon I begin writing the first chapter.

I think you work too hard. Take rest before writing.

She closes the newspaper; the breeze fans his face.

I've had all the time in the world.

American, he thinks; you hear it in the way her voice squeaks, as if a demon were trying to leap out. Impatient. *Get on with it,* Americans always say. She lived three years in Chengdu, teaching English at a shoe factory, and it didn't change her a bit.

So what do you think, Mr. Chen? Will the village system work?

He smiles; this is the way she always is. You ask the wrong person, he says. How can I know about these things?

I follow the old saying: *Lao tou duo jing yan.* The old have more experience.

He laughs. Old or young doesn't matter. Politics I not understand. You ask anyone and get better answer.

Mr. Chen, she says, you know you are a remarkable person.

I am not special, he says. Hong Kong blind people library only have English books, English records. So I learn English. There are many old ones like me. Before library hire Chinese people make recordings.

But you're the only one I know, she says. To me you are special. So I ask your opinion.

He frowns, bunching his eyebrows together. Sometimes he doesn't know what she's getting at. Drink more tea, he says. This is special kind from Yunnan. Good for digestion.

The newspaper rustles again. Let's see what else is going on, she says. A long moment passes; he asks Mrs. Sze to lie on her side, and puts a fresh towel over her shoulder and neck. Under the cloth her skin stretches like a loose-fitting shirt.

The shop door slams; a rough old woman's voice calls out to Lao Jiang in a thick Hangzhou dialect. Outside in the street, a lorry's brakes squeal, and ten horns sound at once: as if someone has smashed both fists down on a keyboard.

All day long his father paces up and down the walkway outside their compartment, or stands at an open window, smoking cigarette after cigarette. From someone he has bought or borrowed a blue jacket and hat, but he still wears the gray wool pants of his suit, and brown leather shoes with thin wooden soles, and his gold-rimmed glasses. Anyone could see that he doesn't belong, the boy thinks, and for the first time he feels a vague fear, fingers pressing gently against his windpipe.

Baba, he asks, why are we going to Lishan now?

Your grandmother is ill. The cigarette crackles as his father smokes it. She is very old. At any moment she could walk to the wood.

To the wood?

She could die. He squats down so that his eyes are level with his son's; his breath smells rotten, decayed. Eyes watering, the boy stiffens his head so it will not turn away.

Do you know what they say about mothers when they die?

No.

If the children are there, then the mother can close her eyes. She can rest. But if the children are not there she can't close them—she'll always be looking, waiting for them to arrive. She dies with her eyes open.

But what about your classes?

I won't teach my classes. Not this year.

What about Mama's job? Don't they still need her?

We think it's better to be in the country this year, his father rasps. In my home place. Chairman Mao wasn't born in the city, you know.

Of course not, the boy says stiffly. Chairman Mao was born in Shaoshan.

So this is like going back to our Shaoshan. Back to our roots. Just so you know that there are other places in the world than Shanghai.

Shanghai, Chen says. Shanghai—he reaches for the counter behind him and misses. For a moment everything is black, as if someone has pressed a hand over his eyes. He lurches, losing his balance, and clutches the edge of the sink. Porcelain smashes near his foot, and his shoe is suddenly warm and wet. He feels her hands on his shoulders.

Lao Chen! *Ni xiao xin dian!*

I'm all right, he says. You can speak English. Is it the teapot?

What happened? Should we call a doctor?

A little dizzy. I didn't eat this morning. Lao Jiang, he calls out. Bring a broom.

Crazy old fool, Mrs. Sze says from the table. Come on! My eyes are killing me.

All right, he says. Xiao Ma pushes him gently from behind; he reaches out and feels the cracked vinyl cushion, and places his hands lightly atop the old lady's forehead. *Aiya,* she murmurs. Better.

Were you thinking about Shanghai?

What?

You said something about Shanghai. Were you having a daydream?

Ah. Yes, it must be. Maybe I hear something on the radio.

A moment passes. She turns the page, and begins to read again.

❖

In the morning the boy opens his eyes and stares at the rusting slats of the bed above them. The sky outside the window is the color of dirty snow. He pulls a hand from beneath the blankets and holds it up to the light; it is as pale as boiled chicken skin.

Wei, his sister mumbles, jabbing an elbow into his side. Stop moving! Go back to sleep.

Jie-jie, he says. Tell me again.

Tell you what?

What you remember.

It's a very small place, she says. Just a bunch of houses with court-yards. And green fields on all sides. It's in a valley, you know, but you can never see the mountains, they're always hidden in the clouds. You won't like it there.

Why not?

The boys are rough. They've hardly been to school at all—they only work in the fields. They like to fight. And they say dirty things all the time.

I've been in fights.

Don't be ridiculous, she says. You shouldn't resist them. Just make friends with the toughest one, the leader. Teach him how to write bad words. Otherwise they'll tie a stone around your neck and throw you in the river.

The boy curls his arms around his stomach and turns to face the wall.

I'm only joking, she says. You take everything so seriously.

The family in the room above his listens to the television at full volume; the sound echoes in the pipes and rattles the windowpanes. In the winter he lies in bed with his headphones on, listening to the radio, but now he opens the window and moves his chair against the wall so that he can lean his head back on the sill and doze to the faint sound of traffic, ten stories below. Coming out of the dream, he hears buses hissing along Nathan Road, delivery trucks creaking on old brakes. Drumbeats from a car stereo. He flattens a hand against his chest and feels his heart reverberate like footsteps in an empty hall.

You will go mad this way, he thinks.

Thirty-one years. And you have not yet leaped from the train.

He lifts his head slightly. A feeling of danger lingers in the distance, a sound barely within range. Old Chen, he thinks, what's wrong with you? What do you have to be afraid of?

Last year at this time, he remembers, we went to the flower market, Lao Jiang and his wife and I, each of them holding an elbow. Peonies, orchids, amaryllis. Buffeted by clouds of scent, like a perfume factory. Last year I wasn't afraid of dreams.

And what has changed recently in your life, old head?

The American girl.

He sits up straight, and then stands, pacing the room, taking deep, angry breaths. It isn't possible, he thinks, she's done nothing wrong, she only has a soft heart. But then there are the funny questions she asks sometimes, the talk of interviews. He laces his fingers together and pulls them apart. Isn't she only a polite girl?

How could she possibly know?

❖

Tell me again what is you study, he says to her. He is washing his hands between customers, craning his neck to hear her over the hiss of the faucet.

Anthropology.

No, no. Your project.

Patterns of adjustment over time, she says. The way people who have survived traumatic upheavals adapt to changes in their environment later on.

Ah.

Taking the situation now in China as an example. The last ten years: 1988 to 1998. And then the decade before that—beginning with Deng Xiaoping's election. And then the twelve years before that.

He feels as if someone has knocked against his chest like a door.

Cultural Revolution time, he says, reaching for a towel. So long ago.

For some people it's as if it were yesterday.

He dries his hands carefully, rubs his palms together and massages his face; there is a sharp pain between his eyes that will not go away. Here there many protests, he says, remembering what Lao Jiang has told him. Riots. Always police in the streets. I stay inside for many days.

Hong Kong was lucky, she says. One woman I met in Wuhan was locked in the same room for a year with her three little sisters. One of them died. One jumped out the window. One went crazy. The man that was responsible is now the head of her work unit. Still lives down the street from her.

Anybody can make a story, he says. How you know who to believe?

I trust them. And I ask lots of questions.

He turns and spreads a new towel out on the table, smoothing its wrinkles. Lao Jiang, he thinks, don't be so shy, come interrupt us. Tell a joke, for once. Talk about the weather. But the shop is quiet and sleepy. A fly drones past his ear.

Let me give you an example, she says. If you were someone I wanted to interview, first I would listen to you tell your story. In a very relaxed way—no pressure, not too many questions. Then I would go around and talk to other people, and see if they remembered things the way you did. Maybe I could find a document, some kind of official record. Then I would come back and ask the hard questions. Connect the dots.

He laughs, too loudly; the sound reverberates harshly in the small room. I think you have a hard time with me, he says. I am orphan, you know. I do not even know when I come from China. In the 1950 nobody keep this kind of record.

Is there any way of finding out? What about your passport?

Why need passport? Where I go?

You never tried to find out about your parents? Where you were born?

He wets his handkerchief under the tap and wipes his face.

It is impossible. But finding out not so important.

I think I could help you, she says. The records must be there somewhere. At least we would know when you came, and who brought you. Maybe even your age.

Xiao Ma, he says. I have no story for you. Nothing tell.

But I might be able to help you remember.

Why? Why you want do this for me?

So that you can know.

Just for me? All this work?

Also for my research. For a—for a later project.

Ah. So I am also subject.

Mr. Chen, she says, I think you have a story that would be interesting to many people. There has been very little work done on the experience of the blind in China. You could bring to light—

This not China. This Yau Ma Tei. Hong Kong.

If I find something, can I bring it to show you?

Maybe better not.

In the front room Lao Jiang is arguing with a customer over the benefits of wild versus cultivated ginseng; the young man has a high, nasal voice, and his Cantonese is slurred and shrill, filled with abuse. *Don't try to cheat me, old man. Look at yourself! Are you an advertisement for your products?* Standing there, listening, Chen feels a slow paralysis working through his veins, as if his blood had turned to ice. We are finished, he thinks. These young people are the voice of the end.

Mr. Chen?

You very determined girl, he says, turning his head to her with an effort. I sorry I can't more—can't cooperate.

I'm not asking for so much, she says, her voice hard and tight. Just the truth. I want to help you find the truth of what happened.

No, he thinks. You want a prize. You want me to be your prize. He clears his throat. You understand, he says. I live here so long, very quiet, and now I am old and no memories. Only food taste good, weather hot, children make too much noise. You ask someone else.

He hears the muffled slap of a notebook closing, a pen clicking shut. Keys jingling as she picks up her bag.

Mr. Chen, she says, you are not a fool. And I am not a fool.

No. He takes a long breath. No, he says. That not the question.

❖

Dadao Liu Shaoqi! Dadao Liu Shaoqi!

Running steps thunder in the corridor. A young man thrusts his face into the compartment. Down with Liu Shaoqi! he screams. His face is smeared with coal dust; his eyes are bloodshot. The boy's father sits up abruptly, banging his head on the bed above. Long live Chairman Mao! Down with Liu Shaoqi!

Long live Chairman Mao, his father says weakly.

Down with Liu Shaoqi!

Down with Liu Shaoqi!

His father's voice rises into a yell and cracks. The young man seizes him by the shoulders. Down with Liu Shaoqi! he screams. Say it! Say it! Down with Liu Shaoqi!

All during the night and into the morning the train fills with them.

Blue jackets, blue trousers, blue caps; the girls have their hair tucked up underneath. Red armbands. Red buttons and pins. Red stars. Some of them have bedrolls or satchels, but most carry nothing at all. They cluster together in clumps of eight or ten; if one is left behind she runs frantically to catch up, butting away everyone in her path. At every station they pull into, there are more on the platform. Some have their own flags: "Nanjing Revolutionary Red Guards Group Five." Periodically they burst into song:

> *The east is red*
> *The sun rises*
> *China has brought forth a Mao Zedong!*

*I want a button, the boy says loudly. Mama, can I have a button?
A girl passing by hears him and bends down, squeezing his arm.
Stand up straight! she shouts. He stiffens, thrusting out his chest.
Salute! His fingers smack his forehead.*

Down with the four olds!

Down with the four olds!

*Here, she says, taking a large pin from her shirt. This is from Bei-
jing. It is in the shape of Tiananmen Gate, with Mao's face in the
middle, and the five stars above, like a crown. His mouth forms an
O. The redness of it burns through his hand; he has never seen anything so saturated with color, like an eye staring at him.*

*Say thank you! his mother shouts from inside the compart-
ment.*

No, the girl says. Say, Long live Chairman Mao.

Long live Chairman—

*Give me that, his mother says as soon as he steps inside the door.
Take that wretched thing off! She sits up on the bed, fumbling with
the clasp, and yanks it away, leaving a small hole in his shirt. And
don't go outside anymore.*

*Xiaomei, his father whispers from his bunk. It's protection. Let
him have it.*

*We don't need protection, she says loudly. Unbound, her hair
falls across her face like a curtain, and she pushes it aside impatiently. We haven't done anything.*

Mama, why can't I—

*They killed Wang Huili's mother, his father hisses. They took her
off a bus on Zhongshan Lu and beat her to death in the street.*

*The boy's hands drop to his sides. He has never heard his father
talk like this: like a street vendor would say it.*

They don't know us, his mother whispers. Her hair has fallen back

in front of her face, and the boy notices now that it is streaked with ash
gray. We're not important enough. Why should we act afraid?

Put the pin back on, his father whispers. Go out there with your
sister and salute.

Minutes later, his face again pressed against the window, he hears
the familiar snick-snick of his mother's sewing scissors, the tearing
sound, and he realizes she is cutting her hair.

That night the Guards sleep crammed together on the floor of
their compartment and in the corridor outside.

❖

The next time she appears it is late afternoon, and he is on his
last customer of the day. Lao Jiang's granddaughter has already
come from school; he can hear her following him around the
shop with little shuffling steps, asking question upon question.
He answers her patiently: *This is wild ginseng. This is deer antler.*
This is pink ginger. At this rate, Chen thinks, she'll be a Chinese
doctor before she leaves primary school.

Would you like some tea?

I'm fine. Thanks.

You are tired, he says. You should take a rest.

It's hot, she says. I always forget how early the weather changes.
April in Hong Kong is worse than August where I come from.

And your work?

She allows the silence to linger while he folds clean sheets and
drops them into a basket between his knees.

Slow, she says. Very slow.

He stands and slaps the massage table cushion with his palm.
Maybe I help, he says. Lie down.

No, no. Thank you, Mr. Chen. I don't need it.

Of course no *need*. I only give very poor massage. But maybe you enjoy. All this time you come here, and not even once you want to try?

A long, whispering sigh. The chair creaks as she stands.

Lie on your back, he tells her. He takes a hand towel, spreads it across her forehead, and puts his fingers to her temples. Fascinating, he thinks. Like touching a television screen: her skin crackles with energy. He makes gentle circles next to her eyes and smooths the creases in her forehead.

Tell me about your home place. Tell me about Oklahoma.

She laughs softly. You really want to know? It's very boring.

I ask question, yes?

She takes a long breath and exhales. I don't know if I can explain it. It's like Mongolia. Very flat, with only grass prairies. No mountains, no trees, no big rivers. Very dry, very windy. Not many people live there. You could say it's like the frontier: *bianjie*. Only in the middle of the country.

And you live in small town?

About ten thousand. For Oklahoma that's medium-size.

What kind of work they have? They have farms?

Oil, she says. They have wells that take oil out of the ground. Well, they *did* have them. Now there isn't much of anything. The economy changed, and the price went down, and everybody went bankrupt all at once. It's a very sad place.

Because now everybody poor.

Because they didn't do anything about it. They knew what was going to happen. And they kept spending their money. You see a lot of houses with four-car garages and only one little Toyota inside. Those people let themselves be victims. She takes another breath. I told you, Mr. Chen. It's sad, but it isn't interesting.

Maybe when you return be different.

Oh no, she says. I'd never go back there. Not in a thousand years.

Turn over, he says. He lays the towel across her shoulder blades and works his fingers between them. Her spine is so taut he can almost hear it hum. *Four-car garage*, he thinks. He imagines the dimensions of a car, and the dimensions of his room. Amazing. To own all of that space and keep it empty.

Soon finish, he says. Then you let me take a little rest.

Of course, she says quickly. I'm sorry. I've taken too long.

Bie keqi. I think it good for you. His fingers make long, soft strokes along her back. Old fool, he thinks, what did you think you could do? Could ten fingers let your demon out? Finish, he says. He pours a cup of tea and sets it on the armrest of the couch, then sits down, leaning his head against the wall.

I don't want to go, the boy says. He is sitting on his bunk, his legs drawn up to his chest. All around him the train makes its cooling noises, little hisses and clanks: they have just drawn into Lishan. The lights in the train have been turned off; his father, in the doorway, is silhouetted in the flickering light of candles and battery torches. Boys in the corridor are playing guess-fingers. Two! Six! Ah, shit! Seven!

What did you say?

I don't want to.

This is your home, his father says. Our home. Grandma is waiting.

How do you know?

Don't be ridiculous. Come on, they won't stop long. Get up!

I can't see anything, the boy says. He presses his hand to the burning-cold window. I thought it would be daylight. I want to see the mountains.

You'll see them in the morning.

Baba—

His father reaches out and pulls him off the bed by the collar.

As soon as they step out onto the stairs they can see the signs, written in huge characters on sheets of newsprint; some of them are lit from behind, like paper lanterns. Immediately he recognizes his father's name, everywhere, on every one.

Chen Zhaolu capitalist roader
Chen Zhaolu May sixteenth leader
Chen Zhaolu China's Khrushchev
Strike down landlord Chen Zhaolu

Arms pull at him from ten directions; his father seems to melt into a crowd of shouting people, Red Guards, soldiers, villagers. Someone loops a string around his neck and suddenly he is wearing a placard that bangs against his knees. He looks down, trying to read the characters, and a hand seizes his hair from behind and yanks his head upright. Put on the cap! someone yells. Put on the dunce cap! Son of a bitch! Son of a bitch!

I knew it! I *knew* it!

What? he starts out of his chair. What is wrong?

You said *gou zai zi,* she says. *You* were a *gou zai zi.* In 1967. That's how it happened.

You make mistake.

The movement to the countryside. You went out from Shanghai—how old were you? Ten? Eleven?

The demon speaks, he thinks. The demon is loose.

You lied to me, she says. Why did you lie?

He drinks from his teacup with a shaking hand, and cold tea splashes his leg.

Zuo ba, he says, loudly, harshly. Sit down. Lower your voice.

Lao Jiang and his granddaughter are quiet. Chen struggles to his feet, feels his way along the wall to the door, and closes it.

I am sick, he says, still holding the door handle, speaking to the wall. You must understand this. When I am standing, when I am walking, I have this dream. All during day I have it. I can not control.

Not dreams, she says. Memories. You have a disorder caused by trauma. Do you understand what that is?

No matter which word.

Mr. Chen, she says, forgive me for saying this. Your face is covered with scars. Anyone can see you weren't born blind.

Ni gen tamen yi yang, he says. You are the same as them. How long did you spy on me? How many times?

The shop is dead silence. Her breaths are quick and jagged; she is crying, he thinks, or about to. Let her cry.

It's in your files, she says. At the Services for the Blind. Where you came across the border, where you were found. I'm sorry, Mr. Chen. I thought that you would trust me. I thought you would tell me yourself.

A fly circles lazily around his head, once, twice.

I can choose, he says. I not choose be born in Cultural Revolution time. I not choose take away from my parents. I not choose leave China. I not choose learn English. But I choose not talk to you.

There's no need to be ashamed.

I not shame. Shame not the point.

You're holding on to it, she says. Let it go. Let it out.

He turns toward her voice and shakes his finger at the air.

There are no words, he says, his throat suddenly dry. No Chinese words. No English words. You can *never* describe.

Maybe not. But it's important to try.

The fly's buzzing makes him dizzy; for a moment he is standing in a strange room, wondering why his cane is not in his hand. Old head, he thinks, why resist her? If you don't tell her now she'll perch on your grave and pester your ghost.

They did it with brick, he says. Sharp corner of brick from inside fireplace. They break off. Take with wok tongs and put in my eye.

Who did? Red Guards?

The boys from the village. From Lishan. After they took us from train.

Just *boys?* Then who told them to?

I tell them.

He reaches up and slams the fly against the doorjamb.

They already knew when we come, he says. They were ready for us. My father beat to death right there, next to the train. My mother they take away and rape. Then she hang herself. This is what I heard.

He opens the door. Across the street, a radio blares a shrill Cantonese pop song. Lao Jiang is pulling down the gate, drawing the padlock chain through the handle. Chen! he shouts. Are you asleep?

Now I go home, he says. You make story. Make paper if you want. You try.

❖

Somewhere near, outside the doorway of the hut, a boy is crying and vomiting on the ground. Ten paces away, he thinks. Perhaps more. Yet the sound is perfectly clear. He is lying with his head resting on the dirt floor, and yet he can hear the wind skittering dead leaves along the ground outside.

I can't, the boy sobs. I can't look at him.

He raises his head an inch.

I'm all right, he says, in a loud, clear voice. It doesn't hurt so much now.

The door creaks.

You're alive, another voice says. We thought we killed you.

Is it day or night?

It's morning.

I need some water, Chen says. Can you bring me some water?

It's here in the basin. I don't have a cup.

I can stand. Give me your hand. Don't be afraid, Chen says. He reaches out, stretching his fingers in the direction of the voice. I can't see. I won't hurt you.

The hand that takes his is an old man's hand, ridged and cracked, the fingers curled stiff.

What is your name? he asks the darkness.

Chen raises his head. It is the strangest sensation: for a moment he wonders whether the ceiling is leaking again. He wipes a finger across his cheek and tastes the salt.

Eyes, you old frauds, he thinks. Good for something all this time.

❖

The last time she appears at Lao Jiang's she remains standing, refusing to sit. I have a package for you, she says. Something crackles in her hands. I'm putting it on the table.

Mrs. Chong, just a moment, he says. He washes his hands and wipes them before reaching for the envelope. Inside is a thick booklet, heavy and stiff; he runs his hand along the spine and feels the Braille.

Blindness and Self-Erasure: A Case Study

I paid to have it transcribed, she says. It's only fair. I realize you may not want to read it.

He opens the cover and runs a finger along the first few lines.

while in other respects a completely normal individual manifests few overt signs of a trauma and recovery

So already you finish.

I couldn't do anything else, she says. I had to.

He slides the book back into the envelope and carefully closes the flap, wrapping the string fastener around and around until no string is left. You are hardworking girl, he says. One day you make a big success.

Mr. Chen, she says, please. I'm sorry you felt that I tricked you. I want you to accept my apology.

Why need apology? he asks. You already get paper. No problem. He wipes his fingers on his jacket and again drapes the cloth over Mrs. Chong's ankle. Automatically his hands set to work, the heels of his palms pressing against the tendon.

I described my methods, she says. And I reported how you responded when you found out. I tried to be fair. I didn't go easy on myself.

Ghost woman, he thinks, bile rising in his throat. Dream-stealing woman. Your *methods.* His hands shudder, and Mrs. Chong starts in her sleep.

Mr. Chen, she says. Are you still angry with me?

Not angry. Maybe sad.

I am also sad, she says. I hoped you would feel better, now that it's over. Now that it's out there.

Out there?

Out in the world. Your story. Now other people can read it and know about you.

At that moment he feels as if he's standing outside on the sidewalk, and the late afternoon sun is warming his neck, his bald scalp. He lifts his hands and smiles in her direction. Not me, he says. Not about me. Only you.

No, she says. I'm only the observer. It's not my experience.

This your problem. You only look with your eyes.

I don't understand.

Oklahoma, he says loudly, as if it were a charm for making things disappear. Maybe you go back there. Maybe you already there, no need to go.

She is silent for so long he wonders if the charm has worked.

I meant well, she says. I came to apologize. You don't have to be cruel.

Cruel? What means cruel? Spy on old man, make notes, is this cruel?

All right, she says. If that's the way you want it. She turns toward the door; he feels a breath of scented air across his face. I'm leaving for Beijing in a month, she says. I didn't want it to end this way. I wanted you to be proud.

He turns away from the sound of her voice and grips the edge of the sink. Proud of what, he wants to ask her. Of these useless bits of meat?

Is that all you have to say? she asks. Is it over?

Over? he thinks. How can it be over?

Yes, he says. It is. Yes. Now please go.

❖

It is true spring, the last days before the air grows thick and oppressive; back in his room, he leans his face out the window and takes long breaths. Old head, you should take walks, he thinks. Like you used to. Take a taxi and go to the Services for the Blind again. He feels absurdly happy, light-headed; as if there was a towel around my mouth, he thinks, and I was breathing through it but didn't know. And now it's gone.

The book lies open on the bed next to him. Every once in a while he turns a page and passes his hand over a line, careful never to read two in sequence. *Typical adjustment procedure, Taylor (1987) indicates that, Evidence of earlier trauma, Manifested in such behaviors as.* It has been years since he has read Braille, but it comes back to him easily. Words, only words, he thinks, they come and go so swiftly. What is the use of them, after all? *Subsequent visits indicated an increased level of.* He laughs, letting his head fall back to the pillow. As if it means something, he thinks. As if I am in there somewhere, waiting to get out.

Now that she's gone, what will you do? he wonders. Will you go on dreaming?

No. I won't walk through that door again.

Lao Jiang's granddaughter will talk to me, he decides. Soon

she will become bored with dried salamanders. She needs some stories in her life. Like this one: how a book can become a bird. He reaches for the report, closes it, turns and flings it out the window; pages snap and flutter as it falls. *Zhu ni zhunyi gaofei,* he thinks. Take life. Now it is time to fly.

For You

January, the depths of winter: nights longer than the days.

Rising at four, the students bow to the Buddha one hundred and eight times, and sit meditation for an hour before breakfast, heads rolling into sleep and jerking awake. At the end of the working period the sun rises, a clear, distant light over Su Dok Mountain; they put aside brooms and wheelbarrows and return to the meditation hall. When it sets, at four in the afternoon, it seems only a few hours have passed. An apprentice monk climbs the drum tower and beats a steady rhythm as he falls into shadow.

Darkness. Seoul appears in the distance, a wedge of glittering lights where two ridges meet.

Sitting on the temple steps, hunched in the parka he wears over his robe, Lewis closes his eyes and repeats to himself, *my name is Lewis Morgan. My address is 354 Chater Gardens, Central, Hong Kong. My wife's name is Melinda.* He tries to see her face again, the way it appears sometimes in his dreams, and usually he can't.

❖

On Monday evenings he accompanies Hae Wol Sunim down the mountain to the local outdoor market. While the monk buys the main provisions of the temple—barrels of kimchi, hundred-pound sacks of rice—Lewis goes to the Super Shop for the extras the international students need. Vitamin supplements. Vegetable oil. Peanut butter. Milk powder. Nescafé. When the old woman at the register sees him, bundled in his gray robe and stocking cap, she puts her hands together in *hapchang* and addresses him as *sunim,* monk, and he has to resist the urge to shake his head and try to correct her. It's all the same to her, Hae Wol reminds him. Remember, she's not bowing to *you.*

Before Hae Wol became a monk he was Joseph Hung, an accountant at Standard Chartered Bank and the secretary of the Hong Kong Shim Gye Zen Center. Lewis met him for the first time two years ago, when a Zen master from Korea came to give a public talk at Hong Kong University; Joseph was the English translator, and afterward, Lewis walked up to him and asked, *can you help me?* For months they met every Friday for coffee at the Fringe Club in Central, and after Joseph left for Korea they kept in touch, using the temple's e-mail account, until he finally told Lewis, *You have to try it for yourself.* He repeated the instructions for sitting Zen, and wrote, *No more letters for six months, OK?*

How are your legs? Hae Wol asks as they load shopping bags into the back of the temple van.

Do you really have to ask? Lewis says. They hurt like hell.

Hae Wol laughs hoarsely. Good answer, he says. One hundred percent. And how does your heart feel?

Worried. Still worried.

Too much thinking. What are you worried about?

I'm afraid I'll forget why I'm here. Lewis puts his hands on his hips and bends over backward, trying to work the kinks out of his spine. But I don't want to dwell on it, either.

So why *are* you here?

He glares at Hae Wol. The small matter of a divorce, he says. That's all.

Wrong answer. The monk folds his arms and grins at him. You're supposed to say, *to save all beings from suffering.*

I'm supposed to lie?

You're supposed to let it go. If you've already made up your mind, not even the bodhisattva of compassion herself can save you.

But I'm not supposed to want to be saved, am I?

Here, Hae Wol says. Try me. Ask me the question.

I hate these games, Lewis thinks. All right, he says. Why are you here?

The monk puts his hands together and gives him a deep, elaborate bow. Two young girls passing by burst into loud giggles, covering their mouths.

For you, he says.

The retreat was Melinda's idea, and that was what made him take it seriously. She'd always been suspicious of Eastern religion—her father had left her family for two years, in the late seventies, to live on a commune that practiced Transcendental Meditation—and she mocked him pitilessly when he brought home *Buddhism Without Beliefs* and *Taking the Path of Zen.*

Then, during their second year in Hong Kong—when the fighting never seemed to end, only ebb and flow—she bought him a cushion and refused to talk to him in the evening until he'd sat for half an hour. This is for my own good, she told him. I don't know what it does for you, and I don't really care. I just need the *quiet*, understand?

He didn't understand: that was the first and last of it. Hong Kong was supposed to be a temporary posting for her, a two-year stint at PriceWaterhouseCoopers' Asian headquarters, with option to renew, and now it seemed that every month her staff was expanded and her division given a new contract. In Boston she had been a star analyst, famous for her uncanny ability to find errors and gaps in a quarterly report; more than once she'd spotted a looming disaster months before it emerged in the market. But the word was that the American executives were afraid of her because she wasn't enough of a *team player*. Expert exile, it was called. If she stayed in Hong Kong, and played her cards right, she finally told him, she would be a division head in five years, and then could transfer herself anywhere—back to Boston, or to New York, London, even Paris. If not, she would have a year of severance pay, and would have to start again at the bottom.

But I can't work, Lewis said, staring into a plate of pad thai. They were sitting on plastic chairs at an outdoor Thai restaurant downstairs from her office. No one hires American photographers here. In five years my career will be over.

And if I quit now in *zero* years my career will be.

And in six months our marriage will be.

You're being stubborn, she said. She lit a cigarette—a habit she'd picked up again in Hong Kong, after quitting six years before—and stared at him, her eyes darting from his forehead to his jaw to his sweater. How many other couples like us live here? she said. Why is it so difficult for you? What's wrong with not working for a little while?

He sat back in his chair and looked up into the glowing haze that hung over the city, blotting out the sky. If I said that to you, he said, you'd call me a sexist bastard.

That's not fair, she said. Being a freelancer is different. You'll always have slow patches.

This isn't a *slow patch*, he said, more loudly than he'd intended; an old woman with a basket of hibiscus flowers, who had been approaching their table, turned and hurried away. Haven't you been listening? If I don't work, not at all, what good am I to anyone? It isn't about the money. I don't want to wake up one of these days and realize I've turned into a hobbyist.

So, she said, I guess this is what they call an impasse.

Is it Hong Kong, he wondered, *or is it what we've known all along, that we're too different, that our lives will never really match?* She had lost weight, even in the last few weeks; in the dim light he could see the faint blue paths of veins along her wrists, and the dark half-moons under her eyes that always reappeared in the evening, no matter how much concealer she used. *Things will be all right*, he wanted to say, but he couldn't see how they possibly would be, and there wasn't any point in lying.

No one could say they hadn't been warned. An office workday ran from seven until eight, and Saturdays were workdays; an *affordable apartment* meant living in a series of walk-in closets; the summers were furnacelike, the winters endlessly dreary; there was no such thing as having a social life. And listen, an Australian woman instructed them at a cocktail party, on her third glass of chardonnay, forget this *international city* claptrap. Hong Kong is one hundred and ten percent Chinese. They may be the richest Chinese in the world, but they still throw their garbage out the window and kill chickens in the bathroom. And you have to accommodate them because, after all, it's their home, isn't it? It belongs to them now.

We're not like her, Melinda said to him, in the taxi, heading back to their hotel. Are we? It's different if you come here because you *want* to. We can explore—we'll make Chinese friends, won't we? And you'll study Cantonese.

Right. Of course.

And you can do amazing work. She rested her head against the window and stared up at the Bank of China passing above them, silhouetted against the night sky like the blade of a giant X-Acto knife. I mean, my god, this is the most photogenic city in the world, isn't it?

I shot fifty rolls yesterday, he said. You should have seen it.

He had wandered the backstreets of Kowloon for hours, a side of the city he'd never imagined: streets like narrow crevasses, the signs stacked one over another overhead, blotting out the sun. Old women bent almost double with age, wearing black pajamas, their fingers dripping with gold. This was what he loved about her, he thought, her absolute certainly about these things, the way she moved instinctively, always knowing that logic would follow.

Now he thinks, *I was young. I was so, so young.*

The pain is always with him: prickling in his ankles, needles in his knees, a fiery throbbing in the muscles around the groin. In every forty-minute session he waits for the moment when sweat beads on his forehead and his teeth begin to chatter, and then rises and stands behind his cushion until the clapper strikes. Walking, climbing the stairs, squatting on the Korean toilet—a dull ache in his knees registers every effort. He sleeps in its after-glow. Make friends with pain, Hae Wol advised him, then you'll never be lonely. And he realizes now that he feels a kind of grat-itude for it, late in the evening sitting, when it is the only thing that keeps him awake.

Whole days pass in reverie, in waking dreams. A camping trip when he was twelve, along the banks of the Pee Dee River in South Carolina. Clay and sand underfoot. Campfire smoke. The rancid smell of clothes soaked in river water and dried stiff in the sun. His best friend, Will Peterson, who insisted on stopping to hunt for some kind of fossil wherever the bank crumbled away. Again he feels the heat of annoyance: the sweat stinging in his eyes, the clouds of mosquitoes that surround them whenever they stop moving. *I haven't changed at all,* he thinks, *I haven't grown: it's all an illusion. Twelve or thirty, it doesn't make any dif-ference. So what hope is there for me now?*

Filling his mug with weak barley tea, he turns to the window, and his eyes become reflecting pools; the blank, paper-white sky, the warm porcelain cradled in his hands.

Twice a week, during afternoon sitting, he descends the stairs and joins a line of students kneeling on mats outside the teacher's room, waiting for interviews. The hallway is not heated; he draws his robe tightly about him and tries to focus on his breathing, ig-noring the murmur of voices through the wall, the slap of an open palm against the floor.

When the bell rings Lewis opens the door, bows three times, and arranges himself on a cushion in front of the teacher, trying not to wince as he twists his knees into the proper position. The teacher watches him silently, sipping from a cup of tea. He is an American monk, a New Yorker, dark-skinned, with watery green eyes and a boxer's nose, twisted slightly to one side. According to Hae Wol he's lived in Korea for twenty years, longer than any other foreigner in the monastery, but he still speaks with traces of a Bronx accent.

Do you have any questions? he asks.

Not exactly.

But there's something you want to say.

I think I may need to leave, Lewis says. I don't think any of this is helping me.

The teacher stares straight into his eyes for so long he stiffens his head to keep from looking away.

Your karma's got a tight hold on you, the teacher says. Like this. He makes a fist and holds it up to the light from the window. Each finger is your situation. Your parents. Your wife. Your job. Your friends. Things that happened to you, things you've done. This is how we travel through life, all of us. He punches the air. Karma is your shell.

And now?

He spreads his fingers wide.

You're sitting still, he says. The hand relaxes. It doesn't know what to do with itself. The fingers get in the way. All of your natural responses are gone.

That's a kind of insanity, isn't it?

Hold on to your center, he says. Pay attention to your breathing. Follow the situation around you. So tell me, what is Zen?

Lewis strikes the floor as hard as he can.

Only that?

Sitting here talking to you.

Keep that mind and you won't make any new karma for your-self.

It's not that easy, Lewis says. I came here to make a decision.

The teacher adjusts his robe and takes a sip of tea. I remember, he says. You're considering getting divorced.

I'm not sure this was the best choice. Coming here, I mean.

Why not?

Well, Lewis says, I'm not supposed to be *thinking* about any-thing, am I?

Haven't you already tried thinking about it? Has that worked?

It hasn't. Does that mean I should stop?

Sometimes you can't solve your problems that way, the teacher says. Your thinking-mind pulls you in one direction, then the other. There are too many variables involved. The most important decisions we make are always like that, aren't they? *Should I get married? Should I move to California?* You try and try to see all the dimensions of the question, but there's always something you can't grasp.

So you're saying that there's no way to solve these problems rationally.

Not at all. Your rational mind is very important, but it also has limitations. Ultimately you have to ask yourself, *what is my true direction in life?* Logic won't help you answer that question. Any kind of concept or metaphor will fall short. The only way is to try to keep a clear mind. And be patient.

Aren't you going to tell me that I have to become a monk?

The teacher grins so widely that Lewis can see the gold crowns on his molars. Why would I do that? he asks. Being a monk won't help you. Do you think we have some magic way of escaping karma? We don't. Nobody gets away from suffering in this world. All we can do is try to see it for what it is.

Lewis rubs his eyes; he feels a dull headache approaching.

I've got a new question for you, the teacher says. Are you ready?

Lewis straightens his back and takes a deep breath.

You say you love your wife, right? What's her name?

Melinda.

You say you love Melinda. But what is love? *Show* me love.

Lewis strikes the floor and waits, but no words come. His mind is full of bees, buzzing lazily in the sunlight. Don't know, he says.

Good, the teacher says. That's your homework. He rings the bell, and they bow.

The housekeeper's name was Cristina; she was paid for by Melinda's company, part of the package that all expatriate employees received. Two days after they moved into their apartment, she arrived with three suitcases and a woven plastic carryall, and occupied the bedroom that Lewis had wanted for his studio. She was polite and efficient, and cooked wonderful food, but the apartment was small even for two people; they took to arguing in whispers, and gave up making love, feeling self-conscious. It took three weeks for Melinda to convince her supervisor that she didn't want or need an amah, even though every other couple in the firm had one, and the contract had to be broken at extra cost, taken out of her salary. When they told Cristina she wept and begged them not to send her away, and they were at a loss to justify themselves. I'll be more quiet! she said. Not even any telephone calls! Finally Lewis threatened to call her agency and complain, and she went to the elevator crying and wailing in Tagalog. All along the hallway he heard doors opening and closing, the neighbors talking in low tones.

Afterward Melinda couldn't sleep for days. She might have been sent back to the Philippines, she said. That's what she was afraid of. Anytime they're out of work they risk losing their visas. Maybe we could have kept her on.

What did you want me to do? Not work?

No, she said. I know. But I don't know how we can live with ourselves.

It isn't our fault, Lewis said. Who thought that an American couple would be comfortable having a live-in housekeeper in a tiny apartment? Couldn't they at least have asked?

Everybody else has one.

Well, I'm not interested in having a servant, Lewis said impatiently. I don't want some kind of colonial fantasy life.

I want *my* life, he wanted to add, *our* life, the one we promised each other, the one we had in Boston. He remembered what she'd said to him in the airport, when they were standing in line at the gate, clutching their tickets and carry-on bags and staring out the window at the tarmac, as if seeing America for the last time: she'd turned to him, wide-eyed, and said, *no matter what happens, we'll still be the same, right?*

That was how it began, he thinks, staring at the ceiling, on the nights when the throbbing in his knees keeps him awake. The things they couldn't have predicted, and couldn't be faulted for. In the first month he visited the offices of a dozen magazines and journals, after sending slides and a portfolio in advance, and found himself talking to assistants and deputy editors who seemed not to have heard of *Outside, Condé Nast Traveler,* or *Architectural Digest,* and who regretted to inform him that there was a glut of photographers in Hong Kong at the moment. For the first time in six years he was officially out of work. On the bus, in the subway, in restaurants, he had moments of irrational rage, hating everything and everyone around him: the women who brayed into their mobile phones; the insolent teenagers with dyed-blond hair and purple sunglasses; the old men in stained T-shirts who stared at him balefully when he paid with the wrong coins. Cantonese was an impossible language: even people who'd lived in Hong Kong twenty years couldn't speak it. He couldn't master the tones well enough to say *thank you.*

But I'm not the only one who changed.

Melinda's cello, which had cost them a thousand dollars to ship, sat in its case in the corner of their bedroom, unopened, growing a faint green tinge of mildew. Her address book hadn't moved from its slot on the shelf above her desk in months. When he called their friends on the East Coast, waking them up after eleven at night, they asked, *what the hell's happened to her?* It wasn't just the seventy-hour weeks; it wasn't the new secretaries she had to train every month, or the global trades that could happen at any hour of the day, in Tokyo, or Bombay, or Frankfurt, so that she often had to be on call overnight. She'd always worked hard, and complained about it, and fought Coopers for every bit of time off she was entitled to. Now they never discussed her schedule at all. If he asked her about vacation time, or free weekends, or made a casual remark about never seeing her enough, she would say, *that's the last thing I want to think about.*

Her face had taken on a kind of slackness, a faint, constant un-happiness, as if no disaster could surprise her. She slept with her knees tucked up to her chest; she was constantly turning off the air conditioner, even when the apartment was stifling, complaining she was cold. Despite the subtropical sun, her skin was becoming paler; she had to throw away all her makeup and start over with lighter shades. And in three months she had gone from two cigarettes to four to half a pack a day.

On a Sunday afternoon in March of that first year he convinced her to come shopping with him at the new underground supermarket in Causeway Bay. She wandered through the aisles like a sleepwalker, picking up items almost at random—a jar of gherkin pickles, a packet of ramen—frowning, and putting them back. Half-joking, he said, I think we've become a reverse cliché, don't you? I'm the bored housewife, and you're the workaholic businessman. Maybe my mother was right.

She stopped in front of a pyramid of Holland tomatoes and turned to look at him, her lips pressed into a tiny pink oval. Just before the wedding, his mother had said to him wryly, *marry a career woman and all you'll wind up with is a career,* and they'd quickly turned it into a joke: when she kissed him, or touched him, she would say, *how do you like my career now?* But the joke isn't funny anymore, he thought, and wished he could suck the words out of the air.

Is that what you really think? she asked. Do you think I arranged it all this way? So that you'd be out of work and frustrated and taking it all out on me?

Is this what you call frustrated? he said. Making a joke? Asking an innocent question every now and then?

I'm not a workaholic. She tore off a plastic bag and began filling it with broccoli rabe, inspecting each stalk carefully for flowers. A workaholic *likes* it.

No, he said. A workaholic can't stop.

She turned away from him, sorting through mounds of imported lettuce: American iceberg, Australian romaine, all neatly labeled and shrink-wrapped.

Can't you ask them for more time off? Lewis asked. Just one Saturday? I mean, it's the same company, isn't it? You're in a more senior position than you were in Boston, and *now* you don't have any flexibility?

Do you know what happened to the Asian markets last week? she asked. Did you even read the papers?

That isn't the issue. That's never been the issue. You'd be working this hard regardless.

I don't know how to explain it, she said. Her face darkened, and she stopped in the middle of the aisle, her shoulders drooping, as if the bags of vegetables were filled with stones. It's different here. She looked as if she would cry at any moment. A young Chinese woman passing them stared at her, then twisted her head to look at him. We have to fight for everything, she said. Clients. Market share. Out here we're not the Big Five. Accounts don't just fall in our laps here the way they do at home. And anyway, the whole economy's in a goddamned meltdown. *Nobody* wants to open up a new account right now.

He should have taken the bags from her hands, and dropped them in the cart; he should have embraced her and said, *forget about shopping, let's get a drink.* Instead, he crossed his arms and waited for her to finish, feeling impatient, irritated at her for making a scene.

And you just don't care, do you? she said. It's not that you want to see me, is it? You've just given up trying, and now you want to go home. Well, it's not that easy. You made a promise to me, and we never said that there wasn't a risk. Hong Kong isn't Boston. If you can't adapt, well, I feel sorry for you.

There was a bitter taste in his mouth. I'm glad you feel sorry for me, he said. I'm glad you feel *something*. He turned around and walked toward the escalator, and though she called after him, *Lewis, wait, I don't know how to get home*, he ignored her and kept going.

At first he thought he would head straight back to the apartment, but he turned right on Queen's Road, blindly, and walked in the opposite direction, into a neighborhood he'd never visited before. It seemed to him that everyone he passed—the old man selling watches from a suitcase, the young fashionable women laden with shopping bags, even the boys throwing a volleyball back and forth—had red, puffy eyes, as if the whole city had been crying. He was walking too slowly; people veered around him, or bumped him with their elbows as they tried to get by.

It would be so easy to leave: to buy a ticket for Boston tomorrow, to rent a studio in Central Square, to make a few phone calls, get some small assignments, to start making a life for himself again. She wouldn't fight the divorce; she would give him a fair settlement, probably more than he needed. A lawyer could finish the paperwork in a few weeks. And she would stay here, getting thinner, smoking more, biding her time until her bosses realized she wasn't going to be driven away. Whatever inertia it was that gripped her now would swallow her whole. *I can't do it*, he thought. *I can't abandon her. I can't shock her out of it*. He stopped in the middle of the sidewalk and stared up at the buildings overhead, looking for a landmark to orient himself. *If I were home,* he thought bitterly, *someone would stop and ask if I needed directions. They wouldn't all stare at me and think, what are you doing here in the first place?*

I have a question, he says to Hae Wol as they are walking through the market, searching for the lightbulb store. What about change?

Change? The monk furrows his eyebrows. Everything is always changing. What kind of change?

Changing yourself. Trying to do better. Not making mistakes.

Mistakes are your mirror, Hae Wol says. They reflect your mind. Don't try to slip away from them.

Enough with the Zenspeak, Lewis says. Plain English, please.

The monk shrugs, and a look of annoyance crosses his face. You have to understand cause and effect, he says. Watch yourself. When you see the patterns in how you act, you'll begin to understand your karma. Then you won't have to be afraid of your feelings, because they won't control you.

I've *been* watching myself, Lewis says. But I keep wondering: even if I understand completely, can't I still make mistakes? How do I know that when I go back to Hong Kong things will be different?

It isn't so much a question of conscious effort. You have to give up the idea that coming here is going to *get* you anything.

Lewis looks around him, at the meat vendors carving enormous slabs of beef, the shoe repairmen, the grandmothers carrying babies tied to their backs with blankets. His eyes are watering.

I keep hearing that, he says, and it just sounds like a recipe for standing still.

No one ever said it was easy, Hae Wol says sharply. It's not like a vacation for losing weight. If you come here looking for some kind of quick fix for all your problems, you're missing the point.

There's something different about him, Lewis thinks. *I'm asking too many questions.* But it's not just that; the monk is nervous, unfocused, even a little jumpy. Every few minutes he scratches the same spot behind his right ear, automatically.

I'll tell you a story, Hae Wol says. Once there was a famous Zen master who visited a temple and asked to see the strongest students there. The abbot said, we've got one young monk who does nothing but sit Zen in his room all day. He doesn't eat, doesn't sleep, and doesn't work. So the Zen master went to see this student. What are you trying to do by sitting so much? he asked. I'm sitting to become Buddha, the student said. So the famous master picks up a brick and starts rubbing it with his walking stick. What are you doing to that brick? the student asks. I'm trying to turn it into a mirror, the master says. You fool, the student says, that brick will never turn into a mirror, no matter how hard you rub it. Yes, says the master, and neither will you ever become Buddha by sitting this way.

You lost me.

Think of a horse and cart. Your body, your actions—they're the cart. Your mind is the horse. If you want to move, which one do you whip, the horse or the cart?

Lewis starts to laugh, shaking his head.

I don't even know why I ask you these questions. You're no use.

It's not me, Hae Wol says. The *questions* are no use. Nothing I can tell you will ever make you satisfied, because all you really want to know is, *will everything turn out all right?*

So what should I do?

The monk stops and draws his fists together in front of his stomach, his *hara*, the center of energy. Tell yourself, *don't know*, he says to Lewis. Say it to yourself, over and over. *Don't know. Don't know.* Don't speculate. Don't make plans. Just accept it: *I don't know.*

Lewis lets out a long sigh.

So we're back at the beginning.

No, Hae Wol says, giving him a playful, twisting smile. Not yet. When you're back at the beginning, *then* you'll really be getting somewhere.

That night he has a dream:

They are in Melinda's apartment in Somerville, the one she had when they met, when she was in the second year of Harvard Business School. The dream begins at their third date, just as it really happened. Late spring, twilight, the sun's last rays streaming through her bedroom window. He is sitting on the bed, and she is standing; they are having an intense conversation about some painter she admired in college, and in the middle of it she begins unbuttoning her shirt, still talking, dropping it to the floor, unhooking her bra, unzipping her jeans. He forces himself to maintain eye contact, because he understands, somehow, that that is what is required; but when he blinks he glimpses the rest of her. The light makes her skin glow like liquid gold. Every movement, every gesture, is like some beautiful kind of dance he's never seen before; he wishes he could see it again, from the beginning; he wants to say, *stop there, start over*. He thinks he is having a religious experience. He thinks, *I have just become a photographer.*

Good for you, she says, still standing there. You just passed the first test.

What test? he asks, trying to look incredulous.

You'd be surprised how few men can hold a conversation with a naked woman.

Stay still, he tells her. Stop moving. Her face blurs; her body vibrates in the air. What's happening to you?

There's this problem with you, Lewis, she says, her voice hollow, echoing, as if they're on opposite ends of a much larger room. You trust me too much. You believe in surfaces. Think about it this way: *You could be making the biggest mistake of your life this instant and you would never know.*

But that's what love is, isn't it? he says. You have to take that risk, don't you?

Not me, she says. That's the difference between us, Lewis. I've read your papers.

What papers, he says. What are you talking about?

A bell is ringing somewhere in the distance, heavy shoes pounding on the stairs. The monk sleeping next to him reaches up and flips the light switch, and he covers his eyes, shuddering.

The morning is cold and overcast, the mountain hidden by low-hanging clouds. In the meditation hall he sleeps, his head fallen to his chest. A monk wakes him with a jab between the shoulder blades, and he struggles to his feet, barely able to stand.

Hae Wol passes him a note scribbled on the back of an envelope. *Demons are everywhere,* it says. *Don't follow them. You're not the only one.*

So I ask you again, the teacher says. What is love?

Today it is cloudy.

The teacher watches him for a moment, lips pressed together, and shakes his head.

Not enough? Lewis asks.

Not enough.

Lewis passes a hand over his eyes.

Love is just coming and going. Like a bad dream.

The teacher picks up his stick and taps him on the shoulder.

I give you thirty blows, he says. You understand emptiness. But emptiness is only half the story.

It's the most incredible thing, Lewis says. I don't feel my legs anymore. No more pain.

You'll want it back, the teacher says. He balances his stick on the ground and leans forward, resting his chin on his hands. Don't linger in hell, he says. Wake up!

In the fall of their second year, with nothing else to do, he decided to write a book proposal, and began reprinting every picture he'd taken in the last six years: taking out hundreds of his best negatives and recasting them with every possible shade and filter. The third bedroom was webbed with drying lines, and the whole apartment reeked of developing fluid. He spent thousands of dollars on paper and chemicals, bought a new computer for digital editing, and still all the new work fell short somehow. In his sleep he twitched and groaned, and Melinda made him move to the couch; then he began working later and later at night, and sleeping in the afternoon. One night, in a fit of rage he kicked the side of his desk, putting his foot through the particle board, and smashed his favorite lens, a 75mm, three-thousand-dollar Leica telephoto. He collapsed into a corner, weeping like a child, and then fell asleep there, in the dim red glow, his head between his knees. Melinda woke him in the afternoon of the next day and pulled him out into the living room, where he sat on a chair with a blanket wrapped around him, trembling.

You need to leave, she said. Sitting in their narrow window seat, her arms wrapped around her chest, as if for warmth, she looked haggard and frail, as if she'd aged thirty years. Go back to Boston if you have to. Or go on one of those retreats you told me about. Two months, absolute minimum. After that we can try again.

Hong Kong isn't the problem anymore, he said. *I'm* the problem. I'm useless, can't you see that? Sending me away won't help.

She leaned back against the window glass, resting her weight against it, as if daring it to break. Her eyes were horribly bloodshot, *like blood in milk*, he thought, for no good reason. I don't know what to do with you, she said. You've got one more chance, Lewis. Do whatever you have to. This paralysis—whatever you want to call it—it's *temporary*, can't you see that?

I can't, he said calmly, scratching his three-day beard. That's why I'm finished. I can't *see*.

Days pass. He sits quietly, following the course of shadows across the floor. At night he tumbles exhausted onto his bedroll and sleeps without dreams. At meals he eats what is given and takes nothing extra, hardly noticing the burning taste of kimchi, the piquant sourness of preserved spinach. He cleans his bowls with tea and drinks the dirty remains without hesitation.

On a certain bright, cloudless day, the warmest yet, the monk who sleeps next to him gives him a note. *Bathe.*

The men's washroom consists of a short hallway, where clothes are left on hooks; a room with spigots protruding from the wall at waist level, low plastic stools and small mirrors, for washing and shaving; and beyond that, closed off by a door, a room with a huge bathtub that stands empty. A sign in Korean and English says, *Conserving water, no use.* It is the middle of the day, and no one else is there. Removing his robes, Lewis winces at the cold, then reaches for the nearest faucet and turns it to hot.

A strange sensation, looking at his nakedness for the first time in weeks. His legs are skinnier than before, his ribs showing slightly. When the water touches his shoulders and face, tears spring to his eyes, and he remembers Melinda showering him in their tiny bathtub, pouring body wash over his head, to his protests, working his shoulders with her loofah sponge. His muscles feel rubbery; he nearly slips from the plastic stool.

A few minutes later, when he turns off the water, he hears someone breathing hard, and close by. A plastic bag rustles. No one has come in, and the door to the outside is closed. He rises from his stool.

Hello?

He stands and opens the door to the cloakroom. Hae Wol looks over his shoulder and starts, dropping a white plastic bottle. Little orange tablets scatter everywhere across the tile floor.

Hey, Lewis says, Joseph—Sunim—I didn't hear you. He moves forward and stoops, suddenly conscious of his nakedness, gathering the pills and dropping them into his palm. What are these, anyway?

Shhh. Hae Wol squats next to him and begins scooping up the pills, pulling the cotton wadding out of the bottle and dropping it on the floor in his haste. Don't say anything about this, he says, in a high, cracking whisper, his eyes locked on the floor. I ask you as a friend, OK? You never saw me here.

All right, Lewis whispers.

After Hae Wol has left, he stands there for a moment, shivering in the blast of cold air from the corridor. Then he pulls on his robes, hardly bothering to dry himself, and leaves, keeping his eyes focused on the floor.

The next Monday they do not speak until they are almost finished loading the van.

Tell me what you're thinking, Hae Wol says finally. Are you angry? Are you shocked?

Shocked? He smiles; he's forgotten how conservative Joseph has always been, even a little naïve, by American standards. I'm surprised, he says. I take it those pills weren't exactly given to you by prescription.

Percocet, Hae Wol says. Painkillers. There's a laywoman who gets them for me. Her husband is a doctor. I went to him when I sprained my ankle last fall, and then I couldn't stop taking them. I just tell her, *I'm still having the pain.* Because I'm a monk, he won't say anything.

That isn't your fault, Lewis says. You need to get treatment, that's all.

Hae Wol shakes his head. No, he says. The fourth precept says *no drinking, no intoxicants.* It doesn't say *except when you really need it.* A vow is only a vow if you keep it one hundred percent of the time. Not ninety-nine percent.

Lewis swallows hard. Like marriage, he says. And yet, here we are.

Hae Wol squints at him with a half-smile, as if it's a joke he doesn't quite understand; then he looks away and nods, and stoops down to lift another bag of rice. You're right, he says, with a sharp, surprised laugh. Whip the horse, don't whip the cart, right?

So the question is, Lewis says, folding his arms to keep them from trembling, what will you do now, Sunim?

What do you think I should do?

Oh, no, Lewis says. Don't ask me that. Who am I to give you advice?

The monk sits down heavily on the bumper, holding out his hands to steady himself. His face is soft and slack, like a piece of rotting fruit. *Who else is there,* his body seems to say. And Lewis thinks, *what am I worth, after all, as a human being, if I can't do something for him right now?*

Give the pills to me, he hears himself saying.

Hae Wol looks up, raising his eyebrows. Now? he says. I don't have them. They're in my room.

You're lying, Lewis says fiercely, his tongue scraping the dry roof of his mouth. He holds out his hand. You want my help? he says. This is the help you get. Give them to me *now.*

Guilt flashes across the monk's face, and he reaches into his pocket. Lewis reaches over and places his hand on the bottle; Hae Wol's fingers tighten, and finally he has to pry it away. Quickly he unscrews the lid, spills the pills onto the gravel, and steps on them, grinding them into the stones.

I can always get more, Hae Wol says unhappily. That doesn't change anything.

Listen, Lewis says. Can you get into the monastery office? Can you send a letter?

Hae Wol shrugs, and nods reluctantly.

I want you to send a letter to Melinda for me, Lewis says. Will you do that? And then you tell that woman that the pain has gone away and you don't need any more pills.

I can't do that. The monk scratches slowly behind his ear, staring at the orange-stained pebbles around his feet. I don't have the strength, he says tonelessly. It isn't going to work.

Do it anyway, Lewis says. Remember what you told me? *Don't know.* Just do it that way.

Hae Wol begins to laugh, his shoulders trembling. You Americans, he says, you take everything so literally. You're really going to force me to go through with this, aren't you?

Yes. Lewis forces himself to smile. You're stuck with me.

And what will you say in the letter?

I'm going to tell her that it's all right to fail, he says. That's not very American, is it? I'm going to say, *you don't really want what you're chasing after.*

That sounds like good advice.

And then chances are she'll leave me.

Don't say that, Hae Wol says, a stricken look on his face. You have to have faith in her. Even if she doesn't deserve it.

He sees her sitting at the tiny dining table in their apartment, opening the letter and scanning it intently, her forehead creased with fear. Her legs are curled up underneath her; she leans forward into the pool of dim light from the window, even though the switch for the lamp is right behind her. Part of her doesn't notice, and part of her wants to stay there, crouched in the gloom, as if she doesn't deserve anything better. It isn't about sacrifice, he thinks, or mortgaging the present for the future. When did she come to believe that hating her own weakness was the only way to survive? *Melinda,* he wants to tell her, *you can choose hap-*

piness, but you have to choose. And relief floods over him like cold rain.

I've been thinking about you, the teacher says, when Lewis enters the room and bows. Something's changed. Your face looks better.

Does it?

I have a little speech I want to give you. But you don't have to hear it if you don't want to.

Of course I do.

Every day, the teacher says, we recite the four great vows: *Sentient beings are numberless. We vow to save them all. Delusions are endless. We vow to extinguish them all. The teachings are infinite. We vow to learn them all. The Buddha way is inconceivable. We vow to attain it.*

So what does this mean? What does it mean to vow to do the impossible?

It means that we're never finished.

Yes. But what else?

It means that the standard is impossibly high. Always out of reach.

Is that the way we practice?

No. I guess not.

Our great teacher says, *try, try, try, for ten thousand years.* Do you understand what that means?

Lewis starts to speak, and shakes his head.

This isn't a game, the teacher says, leaning forward and staring at him. Lewis feels his eyes watering, and tries not to blink. You don't *figure these things out.* The great work of life and death is happening all around us all the time. When do you have the chance to sit back and consider every possible option? You have to *act*.

And what if you're wrong? What if it turns out to be a disaster?

The teacher reaches out with his stick and raps him on the knee.

It already *is* a disaster, he says. Don't cling to some dream of a perfect world. Put down your fear and you can cut a path through the darkness.

Without thinking, Lewis bows, resting his head on the floor, raising his open palms in the air. I'm trying, he says. That's all I can do.

Now you understand, the teacher says. This is love. Go home and take this mind with you.

Before climbing the stairs to the dharma room, he opens the outside door and steps out into the courtyard. It is just sunset, and the sky above the mountain is washed with orange and gold; but in the west a dark line of clouds throws the city into shadow, and the air tastes of snow. He is wearing only socks, and the cold sears his skin with every step. *Is this what hope is like,* he wonders. *How long has it been? How would I know?* He opens the door again and climbs the stairs slowly, staring at his feet, making no sound.

The Train
to Lo Wu

Whenever I remember Lin I think of taxicabs. We spent so much of our time sitting in the back of one, somewhere in Shenzhen—speeding away from the border crossing station, or returning to it. In my memory it was always a bright morning, sun streaming through the dusty windows, or late at night, our bodies striped with the colors of the neon lights passing overhead. We sat on opposite sides of the seat, our hands folded, like brother and sister; she wouldn't let me speak, or even touch her leg. If the driver heard my terrible Mandarin, she said, he and his friends would know exactly who she was: another country girl peddling herself to a Hong Kong man for easy money.

I obeyed her, of course. And that's why I was so surprised the one time she broke her own rule. We had just turned the corner at the Kuroda hotel; we were five minutes away from Lo Wu, the border crossing to Hong Kong. She turned to me and said, If I don't call you this week, what will you do?

I'll call you, of course. Why do you ask?

No. That's not what I mean. What if I never called you again?

She had put on a new shade of lipstick that morning, one I had bought for her; against her skin it looked like fresh blood. It made me shiver.

Then I would come and find you. One way or another.

But you couldn't, she said. If you never called *me*, I could find your number in the Hong Kong directory. I could find your family and where you worked. But what could you do? China is too big. If I disappear, that's it. China will swallow me up.

She was right about the driver: he turned his head toward us as he drove, to hear better, and when we came to a traffic light he turned and gave me a salacious grin. I wanted to curse at him. But all the curses I know are Cantonese, and he wouldn't have understood.

Lin, what do you want me to say? I said. You're right, of course. If you *want* to disappear, you can. One way or the other, it's in your power.

Her eyes widened, as if my answer had made her suddenly angry. What makes you so sure of that? she said. What makes you so confident?

I didn't know what to say. We were pulling into the long line of taxis in front of the station; the street was filled with people hurrying toward the entrance. My legs itched. *I'll see you next week,* I wanted to say, but I knew, without wanting to know, that the words didn't matter. The driver turned around in his seat and looked from my face to hers, eager to hear the last line. I took out a wad of hundred-yuan bills and gave him the dirtiest one.

When you get on the train, she said, it's like a dream, isn't it? As if none of this ever really happened. That's good. You should keep it that way. Sometimes dreams happen over and over again, sometimes they don't.

Lin, I said, that's the most ridiculous—

She opened the door and strode away quickly, pushing through the crowd, like a fish fighting its way upstream.

If it were not for Little Brother I would never have thought about China. I live in the New Territories, not far from the border, and the train to Lo Wu passes through the station I use every day, but I had never once considered taking it there. I don't have any relatives in China—my family has lived in Hong Kong for five generations—and I don't like to travel. I've never had that kind of curiosity. And I suppose I still remember the stories my parents' friends told, about the Communists and the Second World War—stories that gave me nightmares as a child. Rows of bodies and babies impaled on bayonets. You could say that for me China was a place that existed only in the past, but not *my* past, a memory that wasn't mine to have.

My own life is really very simple. My parents died years ago, when I was in college; I was an only child, and they left me a portfolio of real estate holdings, and their apartment in Tai Wo. During the day I manage the accounts at an oil trader in Kwai Hing, and in the afternoon, every afternoon, I take the bus to the Shek O Sailboard Club, at the far southeastern tip of Hong Kong Island. If you've ever taken a ferry or a junk trip around the island you've probably seen me in the distance, crossing your path: a tiny, dark figure attached to a bright triangle of sail, hurtling across the waves like a pebble from a slingshot. This is Big Wave Bay, where the typhoons come ashore, where the world speed record was once set. My nickname is *fei yu,* flying fish, and it's true. Two days out of the water is a lifetime to me.

It'll take two hours, Little Brother told us one Friday night, in the back room of the Sha Tin Bar. Cross the border, change some money, take a taxi, pick up some boxes, and go back home. What could be easier than that?

We looked at him skeptically. Little Brother is the youngest of five friends I've had since primary school—the Five Brothers, we call ourselves—and like a real little brother, he's the wild one: he dyed his hair blond and started racing motorcycles in Form Three, when he was only fourteen. Now he owns his own repair shop in Mong Kok and takes his grandmother to play mah-jongg every Sunday.

What's in the boxes? Siu Wong asked him.

Parts. Honda parts.

Are they stolen?

How should I know? All I heard is that they're there. Half the price I pay for them to come from Japan.

Why do you need all five of us? I asked.

You never know what's going to happen, he said. It's Shen-zhen, isn't it? And I thought we might explore a little bit, since we're there. You know, Hong Kong people live like kings in China. The best of everything. He winked.

I hesitated: it wasn't my idea of a good way to spend a Sunday afternoon in April. But if he wanted my help, how could I refuse? It sounded so easy—all I had to do was bring my passport.

None of the five of us is married. I should have mentioned that.

When you step out of the border-crossing into Shenzhen, at first it seems that the air is full of dust, but actually it's the pollution that gives the light a milky quality, even on the clearest of days. Everything seems oversized: wide, empty sidewalks and six-lane avenues, a train station that stretches across four city blocks, sky-scrapers whose tops disappear in the haze. Even the policemen's uniforms are baggy and loose, as if they were children playing dress-up in their parents' clothes. All around you are things for sale—Nikes, North Face jackets, Tissot watches, new movies on VCD—and only when you move closer can you see the badly photocopied labels peeling off, the zippers hanging loose, the image blurred on the package. If you stop anywhere for too long somebody will push you from behind and snap a few harsh sylla-bles you recognize, but only barely. I studied Mandarin in school, and speak it passably, but still I always remember what my mother used to say, that she could never trust anyone whose voice reminded her of a squeaking rodent, a rat caught in a trap.

All through that first taxi ride I kept my face close to the win-dow, ignoring the conversation, trying to absorb everything I saw. Buildings made of white tile, the kind used for bathrooms, with windows of blue-tinted glass; a woman in a soldier's jacket riding a bicycle, her daughter balanced precariously on the crossbar; a man in an ill-fitting suit and loafers, shoveling coal into a wicker basket. Little Brother standing on a sidewalk, smoking cigarette after cigarette and arguing with the shop owner in fractured Can-tonese. It did no good: the parts had already been sold. I remem-ber looking at my watch and realizing that four hours had already gone by, and thinking that when we arrived back at the border it would feel as if no time had passed at all.

I tell you what, Little Brother said at some point. Let's not make this trip a total failure. I'll take you guys to Club Nikko. It's in the Radisson—we can walk to the border from there.

There's a Radisson here?

Of course, he said impatiently. This is Shenzhen. They have everything.

Later I used to tease Lin about how she looked the first time we met: dressed in a white and baby-blue miniskirt, knee-high boots, and a Löwenbräu hat, a living commercial. She was a bar girl, who swooped down on tables before the waitress arrived, gave out free lighters and coasters, and offered Löwenbräu at a "special price," and she was terrible at it. Her voice was high-pitched and squeaked with nervousness, and she mangled the Cantonese tones; the customers' laughter sent her bouncing from table to table like a pinball. Little Brother was telling a long story about the first time he visited the Guangzhou racetrack, and eventually I lost the thread of it, and leaned back from the table. By that time it was late, and no new customers coming in; she was standing against the wall in back, by the bathroom door, and even across that darkened room I could see her cheeks burning.

Going to the toilet, I said, setting down my beer. Siu Wong, sitting next to me, slapped me on the back. As I passed I glanced at her, and she looked away; tracks of mascara were beginning to run from the corners of her eyes.

Here, take this, I said abruptly, taking a packet of tissues from my jacket and thrusting it at her. She accepted it silently. I went into the bathroom, used the toilet, and washed my hands several times over. When I looked into the mirror my own face was red.

Thanks, she said, as soon as I opened the door, and handed me back the packet of tissues. Where she had wiped around her eyes was now blue-black, and she looked like a panda bear. I feel better now, she said. Everything's OK.

It's not your fault, I said awkwardly, trying to remember the Mandarin words. It isn't your language. Maybe next time try a bar without so many Hong Kong people.

Hong Kong people *tip.*

I must have looked bewildered, because she laughed in my face, with a harsh sound. *Aiya,* she said, you really are one of them, aren't you? Haven't you ever been to China before?

Never.

Well, let me tell you something you don't know. I have a college degree. You won't catch me working in some bar for lowlifes. This is good money.

What was your degree?

Primary school education.

She crossed her arms and turned her head away, glancing at me sideways. *She's waiting for me to laugh,* I realized, and pursed my lips and nodded, as if it were the most normal thing in the world. You couldn't find a teaching job here? I asked.

Are you crazy? A country girl like me, from Anhui?

Maybe I can help. I took a business card from my wallet and gave it to her, and she accepted it formally, with both hands. I have some friends who work in Shenzhen, I said. Maybe they could find you something better. Have you ever worked as a secretary?

She wasn't listening; she was still reading the card, her lips moving silently. *Hah vay,* she said. That's your name?

It's pronounced *Harvey.*

Well, listen, Harvey, she said, turning to face me, her arms still crossed. I won't embarrass you by giving your card back in front of your friends, but I'm not interested in your kind of help.

But I was just—

Are you deaf? Leave me alone!

When I returned to the table Little Brother had already told them the punchline, and everyone was reeling with laughter, clinking their bottles for another round. Siu Wong leaned over into my ear.

You can do much better than that, he said. Why play around in the trash? Just ask Little Brother to take you to Second Wives Village sometime.

It was all I could do not to turn and smack him across the face.

I don't think I was as naïve as I must have seemed to her that day. I knew how many men go over the border on "business trips," and how many Chinese women stay in Shenzhen for years, waiting to be allowed into Hong Kong to join men they think are their husbands. But I'm not the kind of person to connect a face with something I saw on the TV news. And I'd never imagined that someone could look at me that way: as a predator, a slippery eel, as Hong Kong people say. For weeks I thought about her, rewording our conversation over and over, wondering if I could have done anything differently.

I was out sailing the first time she called. When I returned to my locker and checked my pager there was a strange, garbled message: *Club Nikko girl returning best time before 20:00,* and a Shenzhen telephone number. When I called I could barely hear her voice over the blaring music and strange banging sounds in the background.

Where are you?

Never mind, she said. I want to meet you again. I'll be in the lobby of the Shangri-La at four on Friday.

I thought you would throw away the card. After what you said.

I think I might have made a mistake, she said. Did I?

Of course you did.

Just so you know, she said, I don't expect anything from you. And you shouldn't either. We're starting off equal.

What do you mean?

You'll see, she said. See you there. And she hung up.

I'd only been to the Shangri-La in Hong Kong once, for an awards ceremony, but as I remembered it the one in Shenzhen was an exact copy: chandeliers, marble, lots of mirrors, and thick carpet that swallowed the sound of your footsteps. Fancy hotels make me nervous; I always avoid them if I can. Being in one of those places makes me feel like someone has handed me something fragile—a glass bowl, an antique vase—and won't let me put it down.

She was waiting for me at a low table in the lobby, drinking coffee. I'd wondered if I would recognize her again, without the clothes, but even through the outside windows I picked her out immediately. Her hair was piled into a tight bun, and she was wearing a dark green jacket; even without the makeup her skin was as white as chalk. Nothing she did suggested she was waiting for someone. Her eyes rested on the floor; she brought the cup to her lips slowly, as if she had hours to finish it. I'd never met anyone so beautiful in that way, so severe and composed and self-contained.

When I walked up to her she barely smiled.

I'm sorry about the phone call, she said. It was a bad line. I couldn't talk long.

It's all right. As soon as I sat down, a waiter appeared. Coffee, I said. What she's having.

Did it take you long to get here?

No. My apartment is only half an hour from the border. In Tai Wo.

She nodded politely. *She has no idea where that is,* I thought. *Don't be rude.* I feel awkward about this, I said. I don't even know your name.

Bai Ming is my name, she said. But everyone calls me Lin.

Like Lin in the book, right?

She gave me a puzzled look and shook her head.

Lin Dai-yu, I said. From the *Dream of the Red Chamber?*

Lin was my elder sister, she whispered. She died when I was twelve.

I took a sip of coffee and looked around the lobby; in various mirrors, from a distance, I could see ten different reflections of our two heads together. As if we were man and wife, or brother and sister, or a boss and his secretary; as if there were one good reason for us to be sitting at the same table.

I didn't mean to embarrass you, I said. Maybe we should speak plainly. I'm not sure I understand why you asked me to come here. Did you want to find out about a job?

I wanted to talk, she said. I've never met anyone from Hong Kong before—just an ordinary person, I mean. I thought maybe that's what you were.

What do you mean by ordinary?

A person who doesn't want something.

I don't think I qualify for that, I said. Everybody wants *something.* It just happens that I don't come to China looking for it.

She stared at me for so long I shifted in my chair.

What is it that you want?

I shrugged. The same as everybody, I guess. Good fortune.

More money. An apartment on the beach. A car. Good health. A family of my own.

You aren't married?

Does that surprise you? Do I seem married?

No, she said. I didn't think so. But where I come from you would *have* to be married.

I smiled. My parents are dead, I said. So no one's banging on my door asking for grandsons.

She looked down at her hands. Close up her skin seemed thin and almost transparent, like rice paper; there were faint bluish shadows underneath her cheekbones. *Does she not eat?* I wondered. *Or not go out in the sun?*

So now we know one another's secrets, I said, and laughed, or tried to; it sounded more like coughing. That's a good way to begin, isn't it? We can't make any worse fools of ourselves.

You can leave, she said quickly. If you want to. Don't feel obligated to stay.

Not at all, I said. But I have a question for you. Why did you want to meet here? Isn't there someplace less formal?

I come here all the time, she said. It's quiet. It's clean. And there's all these chairs that hardly anyone ever sits in. The waiters all know me—I used to work in the bar downstairs. They don't care if I sit here for hours.

It seems very lonely to me.

That depends on how you look at it. I think it's peaceful.

I put down my cup and studied her face, as if for the first time. To me the word *peace*, the word *ningjing*, has a very specific, private meaning: it means the sound of the sea, of waves slapping against the board underneath me, and the feeling of crossing the bay on a stormy day when no other boats are out, and the water is the color of slate, and I'm all alone underneath a ceiling of clouds. Hong Kong people don't use this word very often, and when they do, you get the feeling they don't know what they're talking about.

I suppose you spend all of your free time in karaoke bars, she said.

No, I said. That's what I was just thinking about. It's exactly the opposite. Do you know what windsurfing is? She shook her head. I'll show you, I said, reaching for a napkin. Do you have a pen?

So I drew her a picture of a sailboard, and explained a little bit about how it's done, the way you stand and hold the crossbar and tilt the sail to turn, the way you feel the wind's changes on your shoulders and calves and the back of your head. While I was talking her eyes began to flash a little, and she started asking questions. Why don't you fall over? What do you do if the wind dies? She laughed and shook her head with exasperation, as if she couldn't quite believe my answers. By that time it was almost five, and we both had to leave; when she asked me if I wanted to meet again I said yes, automatically, and then thought, *this is the first thing that has happened in my life that I could never explain to anyone.*

For the next month we met once every week, on Saturday afternoons, always at the Shangri-La. Once afterward we went down the street to a Shanghai restaurant and ate lion's-head meatballs and Shaoxing pork. I always asked for the check; outside, so as not to embarrass me, she paid me for her half, in old two-yuan bills so soft they fell through my fingers and fluttered to the sidewalk. When I protested, the crinkles of laughter disappeared from the corners of her eyes, and she gave me a cold smile. If you want to see me, she said, you'll let me pay my share.

But it's ridiculous, I said. They won't even take these at the exchange window, do you know that?

She stooped and picked up the bills, bending her knees to one side, and stuffed them into my vest pocket. Keep them as a souvenir, she said. They're not so little to me.

I laughed, but I was the only one.

I would be the first to admit I'm no expert on love. Before Lin I'd had other girlfriends, but really only by accident, and never for longer than a few months. A secretary in another division of my company, after we met at an office party. A friend of Siu Wong's little sister, who asked me to help her with some accounting problems. Every one of these relationships ended with some variation of the same phrase: *You're a nice man, but I don't think this should go any further. This isn't love.* And it was true, of course: I didn't feel anything special for any of them, not even during sex, not even at the moment of orgasm. The whole performance to me was so physical, so lacking in personal feeling, that I always felt a little embarrassed afterward and wished she would simply leave. After a few encounters this embarrassment became so strong that I couldn't even hold a conversation, and so it ended, quickly and quietly, with little protest from either of us.

There was a time in my mid-twenties when I wondered if I was gay, or asexual, if I would be happier as a lifelong celibate or a monk. I even considered going to a psychologist to see if there was something hidden in my past keeping me from being able to love. But I never went through with it. The sad truth is that it didn't bother me all that much. I had my friends; I had my health and strength; and I had the ocean, the waves, and the wind—the one deep love of my life, you could say. You might say I decided to let fate choose for me. Probably, I thought, I *would* wind up married, and a father. But not by my own efforts, not by forcing the matter.

I never once considered the danger of this kind of passivity. I never thought that love would come out of the sky when I least expected it, like a storm on a clear day, and that I would have no choice but to bow down and face it, unprepared.

In all that time I never mentioned Lin to anyone. When my friends at the club asked where I was on Saturdays, I told them I was busy with an extra project at work; if Siu Wong called I said I was too tired to go out. It wasn't simply a matter of embarrassment. Every time I imagined what I would say—*She's very nice, smart; she has a college degree, she's really a teacher*—my stomach rolled up into a tight little ball. *Even so,* I heard Siu Wong saying, *what are you going to do next, live in Shenzhen? She doesn't have any connections—she can't leave. Do you think you can just become Chinese?*

That was the real question, of course. In Lin's eyes I was a nice man who wore tracksuits all the time and made silly jokes in bad Mandarin: all the rest of it, my parents, my job, my friends, were to her like shadows in a puppet show. And to me she was even more perplexing. Her parents were engineers who worked in a state-owned garment factory that made uniforms for the army. During the Cultural Revolution they were sent to the far west, to Gansu, and worked digging stones in a quarry; she was born there, in a mud hut with no running water. What could I ever say about that? All I knew about the Cultural Revolution was from movies.

In the end I did the only thing I could think of: I brought her the first volume of *Dream of the Red Chamber*. In the book Lin Dai-yu is the hero's true love, a beautiful, ethereal orphan whom he is forbidden to marry, because of her poor and inauspicious background. Eventually he is convinced to marry her rival, and she falls ill and dies of grief, but that was irrelevant to me; the first part of the novel is filled with the hero's dreams of her, and poems written in her honor. I gave it to her on a Saturday in March, and the next week it was sitting on the table by her elbow, wrinkled and dog-eared, when I came in.

Have you finished it already?

Finished it? Her eyes were puffy, I noticed, as if she hadn't slept, and hadn't bothered with makeup. I read it twice, she said. I think I don't understand you.

Didn't you like it?

Harvey, she said, she's an *orphan*. She lives far away from her hometown and she knows she'll probably never see the South again. All around her there are fabulously rich people, but she has no money of her own. How did you think it would make me feel?

It's a novel, I said. Not an essay on society. It's a love story.

She pushed it across the table, and it fell into my lap. Keep your novels, she said. I have enough problems.

I turned it over in my hands: the lamination peeling from the cover, the spine folded and broken. Lin, I said, tell me what you want.

She gave me a suspicious look. You mean right now?

In the future. Tell me what you want the most.

She stared down at her hands.

Or else I don't know why I should keep coming here, I said. What good are we to each other? You seem to think that I can't understand you, no matter how hard I try.

It's ridiculous, she said. You'll laugh at me.

The waiter brought our cups of coffee; I took a sip immediately, and burned my tongue. Go on, I said, wincing.

I want to have a kindergarten. She bit down on her lower lip, scraping it with her teeth. Not work in one. I've done that. I want to have a private kindergarten, like they do in Shanghai and Beijing, where the parents pay. That way you can have enough blankets and cots and chairs for every student. You can do painting and music and teach English. And you can get your own cook and have decent food. Only a certain number of students admitted every year.

There's nothing ridiculous about that, I said. How much would it cost?

She looked down at the table, a flush rising from her neck.

It's impossible. They wouldn't let me change my residency. And I would have to buy a new teacher's permit—if they would even sell me one.

Are you sure of that? I wanted to ask, but something stopped me—the way her shoulders seemed to go limp, or the bright spots on her cheeks. Thank you, I said. I'm glad you told me that.

Why?

Because I don't want to leave you.

She furrowed her eyebrows; for a moment I thought she hadn't understood me.

We can't talk this way. You don't know what you're saying.

I think we have to, I said. I don't think we can go on this way much longer.

You don't understand, she said. There's no other way. There aren't *options*.

Maybe we should go someplace where we can talk alone.

I live in a dormitory, she said. It's a women-only building. If anyone saw me with you I would be evicted overnight.

Then maybe we should—

Go to a hotel room?

I don't want to be vulgar, I said. I just want to spend more time with you.

There are places, she said, pressing her lips into a line. But you have to pay by the hour. And sometimes they don't clean the sheets in between.

Fine. Then I'll spend the night in a hotel, and we'll go out together for dim sum in the morning.

She shook her head. Understand this, she said. It isn't that I don't want to. But in Shenzhen, if you pretend to be a whore, you are a whore. And I won't do that. Not even for a second.

You don't have to, I said, tightening my fists under the table. It won't come to that.

It took me two weeks to find a solution. When I first told Little Brother what I wanted, he laughed so hard I took the phone away from my ear, and shouted at him to be quiet and get serious. Two days later, he faxed me a list of flats in Shenzhen that could be rented by the night, the week, or the month, no names taken, and no questions asked.

Don't you have any friends in Shenzhen? I asked him the next day. I'm looking for a—a more personal arrangement.

What does that mean?

I don't want to pay, I said. Not directly. Maybe you could give him a gift, and then I could reimburse you. But I don't want to have to give money directly. I made a promise.

You are a strange one, he said. What kind of girl is this?

She's very principled.

And you're going behind her back?

There's no other way. I'm not happy about it.

Whatever you say, flying fish, he said. All that salt water finally went to your head. I'll find you something.

When I told Lin about it, at first she refused. You're missing the point, she said. I told you already. If you pay for this, you might as well pay for everything. I won't belong to anyone, don't you see?

I'm not paying anyone anything, I said. Someone's doing me a favor. There's no money involved.

But it's *yours*. It's your friend. It's your power to say yes or no.

Then you decide, I said. I'll be there on Saturday. You can come or not.

That was how I came to stay at the apartment on Nanhai Lu. It was in a new building, painted white, at the end of a little strip of land that jutted into Shenzhen Bay. The rest of the strip was taken up by a hotel development that had been abandoned, leaving only concrete foundations and rusted metal prongs jutting into the sky. The apartment was on the fourth floor, and the bedroom windows faced the water; there were times when I woke up there and gazed out across the bay, forgetting where I was.

Sometimes Lin came on Saturday afternoons, left in the evening for work, and didn't return; but most weekends she came briefly on Saturday and all day Sunday. I took things as slowly as I knew how: we watched movies on the VCD player, played guess-fingers and Go, and listened to our favorite CDs, Chopin and Faye Wong and Kenny G. She taught me how to steam a whole fish with sweet wine sauce; I made her macaroni with ham and milk tea.

It sounds ridiculous to say so—especially now—but I think of those days as some of the happiest of my life. When the door closed, Lin became a different person. She took long showers, filling the apartment with steam, and came out of the bathroom barefoot, wearing a Polo sweatsuit I had bought for her at the border. The apartment had a set of two plastic-covered couches in the living room; she liked to lie back on one and prop her legs up on the other with her eyes closed. This reminds me of home, she said. Room to stretch out. No one watching you all the time.

Take off the plastic, I told her once. The landlord won't mind. It's supposed to come off.

Plastic is fine. She slapped the cushion for emphasis. It's *clean.* It doesn't get wet. It doesn't mildew.

But it's uncomfortable. Your legs stick to it.

Don't worry, she said softly, almost whispering. She was drifting off, as she often did; some Sundays she would nap for two hours in the middle of the morning. You know, Harvey, she said, her voice wavering with sleepiness, you're too kind. You're too good a person for this world. You should be more sensible.

I'm not so kind to everyone, I said. Only to you.

That's what I mean. I'm not such a wonderful person. I don't deserve it.

I don't believe that.

Do you know how I got to Shenzhen? She sat up, wiping her mouth on her sleeve, and curled her legs under her. Have I ever told you this story?

No.

I bribed a transit commissioner in Zhengzhou, she said. To get a residence permit. He wanted two cases of Marlboros and a bottle of Suntory whiskey. I got fake cigarettes from a guy I knew in my college. The whiskey was the hard part. I had to save up for six months to get one small bottle.

It's an unfair system. Why should you feel bad about that?

Not about that, she said. He was a huge, fat man—you know, so fat he could hardly fit behind his desk. His head looked like a balloon; it was perfectly round. And he had a mustache that grew black only on one side. When I gave him the cigarettes he opened the carton and started smoking one after another, at the same time he was filling out my form. He left these oily fingerprints all over it. And then, two weeks later, I heard he had a heart attack. Just fell over at his desk. And when I heard about it, I just started to laugh. I could see it so clearly. He was sucking those cigarettes so hard I thought he might keel over when I was there.

She giggled a little, and covered her mouth, but not so much that I couldn't see her broad smile. You see? she said. Do I deserve your kindness, Harvey? A man dies and all I can do is laugh.

Lin, I said, I don't blame you. If I were in your place I would have felt the same way.

But you weren't, she said. You've never had to do anything like that. Why should you have to sympathize with me? I've never been able to understand that. I'm not so special. Why do you have to go to all this trouble?

Maybe because you don't want me to, I said. I had meant it to be playful, but as soon as the words came out of my mouth I realized it was the truth. You've had so much unhappiness in your life, I said. I don't blame you for doubting me. But I *want* to understand. Doesn't that count for something?

She shook her head. You can't, she said. It's pointless to try. It's masochistic. You know that, don't you?

Tell me to leave if you want, I said. I felt suddenly angry; all the warmth had drained out of her face in an instant, as if she had willed it to. We're not as different as you think, I said. My parents are gone. I know what it's like to wake up and not know whether I'd rather be dead or alive. Don't tell me that just because I have money I've never suffered.

Stay, she said. She reached up and motioned for me to come to her. I sat down on the couch, and she leaned over and rested her head carefully on my shoulder. Let's not talk, she said. Talking just reminds me that I have to leave.

But otherwise we'll just be strangers.

We're strangers anyway, I expected her to say. She put her hand on my elbow, as if to keep me there. In a few minutes I heard her slow, steady breathing, and realized she was asleep.

Each time she came we kissed only once, just before she left, and over the weeks the kisses became longer and longer, until she dropped her bag of work clothes and stood in the doorway with her arms around my shoulders, tears starting in her eyes.

You don't have to go, I said. Tell them you were sick.

I'm supposed to be saving money, she said. Instead I'm spending it. If I don't show up they'll fire me then and there. In Shenzhen you don't get second chances.

You can find something better, I said. You're spending everything you make on taxis. It doesn't make any sense, Lin.

I told you. I warned you that it wouldn't work.

Let me help you, then.

She pressed a finger to my lips.

My life is so little to you, she whispered. A snap of the fingers.
I'm the dust you shake off your shoes.

Do you think that's what I meant?

She shook her head. You don't have to mean it, she said. It
just *is*.

It was June. In the evenings after she left I went for walks along
the concrete seawall that overlooked the bay, watching the sun
melt through layers of haze. The water there was clotted with
sewage and the shiny bellies of fish; without wanting to, I imagined myself paddling through it on top of my sailboard, and felt
a shiver of nausea and disgust. *That isn't fair,* I thought. *There's
always garbage on the beach at Shek O.* I turned to the east and
looked up at the skyline, or what little of it I could see through
the smog: a jumble of tall spires and cylinders and shining glass
tower blocks, some of them copies of buildings in Hong Kong,
others probably copied from buildings elsewhere in the world.
Why is it that Shenzhen doesn't look quite right, I wondered. *Why
does it seem like such a mirage, as if I might come back next week
and find it gone?*

We slept together for the first time on the night of July 1, the
first anniversary of the handover, of Hong Kong returning to
China. From Nanhai Lu we could see the fireworks over downtown
Shenzhen and over the Tsing Ma Bridge in Hong Kong, and
on satellite TV we watched the small crowds gathered in Statue

Square, waving the new Hong Kong flag—the one with the purple flower, the bauhinia. The joke is, I told her, that it's a hybrid flower, and it's sterile. Produces no offspring. But she didn't laugh. In the flickering light of the screen her face was inert, unmoved; nothing I did made her smile.

I'm sorry, she said. I'm just tired.

You need to look for another job. A day job. This work isn't right for you.

I don't see what they're celebrating, she said, nodding at the screen. Hasn't it been a terrible year? What about the stock market crash?

They're celebrating the future, then. Things will get better.

The future, she said. What a luxury.

I turned off the TV and we sat slumped on the couch in the dark.

I'm sorry. She touched my knee. I feel like I've poisoned you.

We have to forget all this, I said. Can't we just be *us*, just once?

She reached for my hand and squeezed it, hard. I want to, she said. Try to make me forget.

When it was over she folded herself against me, limp, like a body washed in by the tide.

I have an idea, I said the next morning, bringing her a cup of tea in bed. I want you to hear me out. Will you listen?

She nodded, brushing hair out of her eyes.

I've been reading some articles about immigration, I said. We both know there's no way to move you forward on the list for Hong Kong. And I can't legally change my residence to the mainland, even if you wanted me to. But there's nothing to stop us from simultaneously emigrating to a third country.

But—

I raised my hand. There are two options for us, I said. Canada and Australia. Both are expensive. I would have to sell my parents' investments. And we would probably have to wait two or three years for you to get a visa. But that's it—three years at the most. You could start a Chinese kindergarten in Toronto or Vancouver or Sydney. It wouldn't be so hard—I could help you.

You would do that? Leave Hong Kong for good?

Not necessarily for good. Once you're naturalized in another country we can move back to Hong Kong if we want to. We'll keep my apartment and rent it out.

She drank her tea in one gulp and set the cup down. You've figured everything out, she said. Haven't you.

It's not so difficult. People do it all the time.

Of course, she said. People buy wives all the time.

Her eyes were bloodshot, and there was a streak of rouge smeared across her nose. And I felt I couldn't tolerate her stubbornness for a moment longer. It seemed perverse, almost artificial, and I felt myself getting angry, a rim of hot sweat around my lips.

The rest of the world isn't Shenzhen, I said. You don't have to see it that way. *We* don't have to see it that way. Once you've left China everything will be different.

She gave a small cry, like a cat when you step on its paw, and reached over and slapped me across the face. Don't tell me about the rest of the world! she shouted. Don't tell me what you can do for me. Is that what love is? She moved to the other side of the bed and stood up, winding the sheet around her. No more, she said. I'm almost out of money. I have to move out of my room.

You didn't tell me that.

I'm getting rid of my mobile, she said. I'm leaving my job.

What will you do?

Don't ask me that question.

Lin, I said, don't I deserve an answer?

She turned to the window, covering her face with her hands, the sheet sagging around her ankles. You should forget about me, she said hoarsely, her voice muffled in her palms. I warned you. You should never have expected anything from me.

I don't believe you, I said. I know what you want. You only have to be brave and want it *enough.*

She took a corner of the sheet and wrapped it again around her chest, and blew her nose with her fingers, the way farmers do. It isn't a question of bravery, she said. You still don't understand.

I blinked my eyes once, twice; the room seemed to bend around me, like a reflection in one of those funny mirrors at Ocean Park. Lin, I said, it doesn't matter who has the money and who doesn't. If I were in your position—

If I lived in Hong Kong, you would never have noticed me, she said, turning from the window. You wouldn't have looked at me twice. Isn't that true?

No, I said, but I felt a sagging weight in my chest, as if I had swallowed a stone. Of course it was true. I saw myself again in the dark back corner of Club Nikko, handing her a packet of tissues, a business card—when would I have done that, in my normal life, with a stranger? *It isn't important,* I wanted to say. *How can it be so important?* But the words wouldn't form on my tongue. I saw my face as she must have seen it: my eyebrows tilted in concern, my mouth slowly forming the syllables, as if I were talking to a child. I hadn't meant to sound that way, I thought. But how else could she have heard it?

Pity isn't love, she said, her voice dropping to a whisper. It doesn't turn into love. Maybe I thought it could, but I was wrong. I'm sorry if I deceived you.

This can't be the end, I said weakly. I sat down on the edge of the bed, steadying myself with my hands; the floor seemed to fall away from me, curving into the trough of a wave. For a moment I thought I would be sick. *You are making a terrible mistake,* I wanted to shout. *You'll always regret this.* But I knew how she would respond. *I made that mistake already.*

I think you're lying to me, I shouted at her suddenly. I wasn't even aware of what I was saying; I only felt my shoulders clenched together, as if I was expecting the ceiling to fall. You're not really out of a job, are you? You're just sick of me and you want someone else. It's a convenient excuse, isn't it?

She turned and stared at me, and a shiver of recognition ran down her body: as if I had confirmed something she had always known. I'm going home, she said. Back to Anhui. Maybe I'll get a job. Probably not. I don't care if I have to eat rice out of a hole in the ground. At least I won't be one of those women who sits in a villa and waits for a man, like a wind-up toy. I may go crazy, but not that way.

We took a taxi together from Nanhai Lu into the city, and at a street corner, just blocks away from the border, she told the driver to stop and got out quickly, without saying a word. Hey! the driver shouted. Pay your fare!

It's all right, I said. I'm paying for both of us.

As I walked to the border terminal the clouds were beginning to break up, and the sidewalks glowed in the glaring sun. Twenty minutes later, when the train pulled out of the station on the Hong Kong side, I rested my forehead against the cool glass of the window and closed my eyes. I knew exactly how I wanted to remember her: sitting on the plastic couch, her feet propped up, her hair still wet from the shower, laughing at some inane romantic comedy on the TV. I strained to fix the image in my mind, but already it was difficult to recall the details: what did she do with her hands? How did her voice sound when she spoke my name?

If I disappear, that's it, she had said. *China will swallow me up.*

Finally I gave up and opened my eyes.

When you take the train south from the border into Hong Kong, after you pass the small town of Sheung Shui, the countryside opens up into a lush valley, a lowland forest dotted with small farms that climb the sides of gently sloping hills. This is the valley of Fanling. In all my trips past this place I had never seen what I was passing: a hundred shades of green so rich and deep that it hurt my eyes to look at them. In the colonial days, I read once, the English governors and magistrates had huge estates in Fanling, and they played a game where they released a fox and then chased after it with horses and a pack of dogs. All the animals had to be imported from England—even the fox! But it was worth it to them, because it was the same game that they played at home in England, and they wanted to forget for a morning that they were here instead of there. I wondered what it would feel like to ride a horse through that incredible landscape, so green that it hurt your eyes to see it, and whether one of those Englishmen might have slowed his horse for a moment, and breathed the air, and felt in that instant that he belonged *here*, on the other side of the world from where he was born. I raised my head from the window, and the faces of the other passengers dissolved, as if I were looking at them from underwater; and I whispered to myself, *peace, peace, peace.*

The Ferry

T his is what it's like to be a freak, Marcel thinks. He strides across the empty arrivals hall, thrilled to be standing after a sixteen-hour flight, and the woman in the pale green uniform at the passport desk tilts her head back and stares at him, openmouthed, as if he has just swooped down from the air. Her lips form a single syllable: *Wah.* It's like a chorus: the stewardesses, the pudgy kids in tracksuits, the old women in embroidered jackets look at him and say it immediately, involuntarily. That's me, he says to himself, folding back the cover of his brand-new passport, looking around for the signs to the baggage claim. I'm Mr. Wah.

Hello? A hand touches his sleeve; he flinches and turns around. A young Chinese woman with silver spiked hair gives him a nervous half-smile, giggles, and covers her mouth. Excuse me, I wonder if you please sign autograph? She presents him with an open magazine, a picture of a basketball player in mid-flight over the basket, surrounded by Chinese characters.

But that's not me.

She looks confused. Sorry? she says. Not you?

No, he says. I'm flattered. That's Alonzo Mourning.

You basketball player?

No, he says. I mean, sure. I play basketball. But I'm a lawyer.

Oh, she says. OK. But she remains there with the magazine folded, expectant.

So that's why I can't sign this, right? You don't want *my* autograph, do you?

Her eyebrows pucker. Sorry, she says. Don't understand.

You don't—for God's sake, he thinks, make the woman happy. OK, he says. Give me the pen.

Peace, he signs, *Marcel Thomas.* But he scrunches up the words, and thinks, she'll never know the difference.

Hong Kong is like no place he has ever imagined. Green hillsides rising out of a steel-colored sea. Rows of identical white apartment blocks that seem to sprout from low-hanging clouds, like mushrooms after rain. When he steps outside the airport terminal the air sticks to his skin, and he feels queasy, his joints rubbery, a bad taste in his mouth. He'd give anything for a shower. Thirteen thousand miles, he thinks, staring at the curving aluminum handrails on the escalator, the green-tinted glass walls of the taxi stand, as if looking for evidence of that fact, some basis for comparison. Thirteen thousand miles from San Francisco. This. And this. And me.

He falls asleep on the long ride into the city, lying across the backseat with his head propped on his garment bag. When the taxi jolts to a stop his eyes open and he sits up carefully. The car is surrounded by people rushing past, bumping up against the window, and he hears a muffled roar: voices, horns honking, music blaring.

What is it? he says. Is it a riot?

Yih ging lai dou ah, the driver croaks. Causeway Bay. Excelsior Hotel, OK?

When he steps out into the street, he finds himself staring down at a sea of black-haired heads, none higher than his chest. People moving in every direction, weaving, colliding, clutching shopping bags and mobile phones and children; no one looks up at him here. A van turns the corner with brakes squealing, and they scatter out of the way; *like ants,* he thinks, *like cockroaches,* and feels ashamed. He makes his way across the street, holding his bags shoulder-high, as if crossing a river. Without quite knowing why, he holds his breath until the hotel's revolving doors close behind him, and then releases it with a gasp.

There's no place like it on earth, Wallace Ford tells him later that evening, on the outdoor patio at the American Club, twenty-two stories above Central. From his seat Marcel can see the shining columns of office buildings crowded close together, and between them, the dark shadow of Victoria Peak. The glow of the city turns the sky dusky orange. There's an otherworldly quality to it, he thinks, as if Hong Kong were one of those cities in science fiction movies, where everyone lives far above the ground. It wouldn't surprise him to see a spaceship passing silently among the skyscrapers, or a white robot coming out to serve them drinks.

You take New York, Ford says. San Francisco. L.A. Chicago. Even London and Paris—none of it compares to this. The Chinese were living in cities before anybody else on the planet. They've got it figured out. It's not always pretty—or at least *we* don't think so. But it works.

He sits back with a grunt of satisfaction and drains his glass. Fifty-three years old, Marcel remembers, and his skin glows like polished copper; he wears a cream seersucker suit, a crisp tailored shirt, and a new pinky ring, a ruby the size of a fish's eye. Marcel hasn't seen him in five years, since before he was hired at Peabody Stein Loeffler; it was Ford who gave him his final interview, who motioned him to shut the door to his office and said, confidentially speaking, from one brother to another. Marcel doesn't remember all of it—a torrent of words, as if Ford had been waiting for years for the right young candidate to appear— but one riff has always stayed with him: *Anticipate the next move. It's the key to good law and it's the key to surviving in this firm. Always be planning. Always listening. Never act until you understand the whole field; and then strike before anyone notices. Work in the small hours. Let the others wake up to the bad news.* He remembers sitting on the edge of his chair, trying to keep up, nodding at the appropriate places. A few times he caught himself thinking, *is this for real?*

It wasn't until his first day on the job that he heard Ford had transferred to Hong Kong, almost overnight, without a farewell party or even so much as a good-bye letter. He was disappointed, momentarily, but then felt a strange surge of relief. *He can't protect me,* he thought, *but he can't make me his errand boy, either. Better not to be anyone's protégé.*

I think you're going to like it here, Ford says, catching his glance and holding it for a moment. You like Chinese food?

I grew up on it, Marcel says, remembering the Fortune Kitchen, across the street from his old apartment house in Yonkers. Somehow it seemed there was always a container of sweet-and-sour pork dripping red sauce on the kitchen table, a packet of egg rolls in wax paper in the fridge. Egg foo yung, he says. Shrimp lo mein. All that good stuff.

You can forget about that. Ford leans forward. I've got a woman who cooks for me, he says. She makes food you won't believe. None of that Happy Delight stuff—everything's fresh, no MSG, no chow mein. She's got me eating it morning, noon, and night. No more doughnuts in the house, no potato chips. I feel like I did when I was twenty-five. No. Better than that. How long are you staying?

Not long, Marcel says. Cold spreads across the bottom of his stomach. They want me back for a deposition on the seventeenth. Next Monday.

Ford shrugs. Not bad, he says. Not bad for a young comer who wants to make partner. We'll make it worth your while. There's some people I definitely want you to meet.

Marcel has to glance away for a second. Another look into those eyes, he thinks, and I'll be telling the whole story, from beginning to end. The lights inside the club have come on, and through the sliding glass doors he can see the crowd gathered around the bar: young, blond, tanned, thin briefcases, martinis, cigars. A few faces he ought to recognize, from Williams or Choate. Can I ask you an honest question? he says. How can you stand it?

You mean the white boys' club inside?

I mean being the only one, he says. Sticking out all the time.

In the airport I felt like I was in a museum display. Some woman thought I was from the NBA. Wanted my autograph.

I'll be honest with you, Ford says. Most can't take it. I've had boys making monkey noises at me on the subway. Sometimes babies cry when they see you. Sometimes they'll pretend not to understand your English. Or make up some excuse: *only Chinese menu,* or some such thing. I've seen lots of brothers come out, and most of them leave after a year or so. And it's too bad. Because they don't understand the underlying principle.

And what's that?

Ford takes a heavy gold pen from his pocket and flattens a cocktail napkin on his palm. I learned this from a friend of mine, he says, drawing carefully. A box with a cross inside it, with a pair of legs underneath, it seems, and a few squiggles attached to the top. This is the Chinese word for foreigner, he says. *Gwai.* It literally means "ghost." Or "demon." Now, usually when they say *gwai* they're thinking of the white man—the white ghost. But actually a ghost is anyone who's not Chinese. White ghosts, red ghosts, black ghosts. He looks up at Marcel, and from his expression Marcel can tell that his attempt to suppress a look of disbelief has failed. It means you don't really exist, he says. Sure, you might run into a little trouble once in a while. But fundamentally you don't matter to them. White people, black people—it's all the same. You're not on their radar screen. They'll make deals with you, sure. They'll take your money. But otherwise you might as well not be there at all.

It sounds like a lonely way to live, Marcel says. He tilts his head at the crowd in the bar. No wonder they stick to their own. You wouldn't know it's not Manhattan.

It can be, Ford says. But that's not necessarily such a bad thing.

On the way back to the hotel Marcel stops the taxi on Kennedy Road in Wan Chai, intending to walk the rest of the way. The driver gives him a knowing smile, and when he steps out of the car he realizes why: the street is a long line of girlie bars, with neon signs blinking overhead. *Hollywood Club. Midnight Sauna Massage. La Fleur de Paris.* He remembers, now, his uncle Bill telling a story of how he stayed in Wan Chai on the way home from Vietnam and gambled away a thousand dollars in a single night.

Hey! an old woman shouts at him in a hoarse voice. Michael Jordan! Hey, over here!

He ignores her, and takes the first right turn, walks a block, then left, and finds himself on a bustling market street. Stalls piled with mounds of oranges, cabbages, mushrooms; dried squid hanging like fans from a wire. The air is filled with a sharp, sour smell, of fish and dirt and rotting vegetables; he finds it oddly comforting. In the next block he sees a newsstand tucked into an alleyway, and stops, looking for an English newspaper. Everything in Chinese: fashion magazines, comic books, racing sheets, even *Time* and *Newsweek*. Each character is like a little map, he thinks, like a maze; how can anyone read so many at once, and not get lost? He stares at one magazine after another, and a strange sensation comes over him, prickling the back of his neck.

Déjà vu, he thinks. It's been years since he thought about his dyslexia; he was lucky, diagnosed early, and his parents fought the schools for special classes and a private tutor. By high school it was under control, and in college it had all but disappeared. But in law school, during exams, he had a recurring dream of picking up a newspaper, a textbook, and finding the words garbled, illegible. Strange, he thinks, being reminded of that here.

In his room, in a folder marked *Confidential*, is the resignation letter Wallace Ford has to sign, and a stack of papers detailing severance pay, company holdings, disclosure and confidentiality agreements, pension and annuity plans. On the plane, he glanced through them one last time and even now, thinking about it, he has a strange sensation of walking on a balance beam and reaching a foot mistakenly into midair. No one should ever have to fire a partner, he remembers Paul Loeffler saying. It goes against everything we believe in. I'd go myself, but it's a busy time. And I think that he'll appreciate it coming from someone he had a close relationship with.

The numbers on the balance sheet were undeniable; the Hong Kong office was hemorrhaging money, billable hours in decline for three quarters in a row. *Wallace Ford is a great lawyer.* He heard that line so many times, in so many different apologetic tones. *But he's no administrator. He has his enthusiasms, his pet projects. It sounds to me like he's gotten in over his head out there. Bank accounts in Vanuatu? Does he want the SEC after us?*

He would have believed it, too, if Wanda Silver hadn't cornered him in the office kitchen late one Friday afternoon, when everyone else had gone home. Marcel had never known what to make of her: a woman older than his mother, with silver streaks in her curly hair, who wore tie-dyed jumpsuits, batik headbands, and bright bangles on her wrists. There was a rumor that she had spent six months in jail back in the seventies, after chaining herself to the gates of the Livermore Laboratory; yet she had been the firm's office manager for thirty years, and held the keys to the firm's safe-deposit boxes, filled out the paychecks, and knew all the passwords to the computer network.

I heard something important, she said, coming in behind him and closing the door with a discreet click. They're sending you to Hong Kong, Marcel, right?

So I've been told.

And Wallace is out?

He turned to face her. Her eyes were bloodshot, and her lips drawn tight, as if she'd been crying. He looked at the clock on the wall above her, and watched the second hand slide past fifteen, then twenty. Wanda, he said, what do you want me to say? I didn't make the decision. It's not my department.

I don't know, she said. I don't know you, Marcel. And I've never really known what to do with kids your age. Pardon my condescension. Young men. So I'm going to assume you're not as naïve as you sound. I'm going to assume you can guess why Wallace Ford was made a partner of this firm.

Marcel stared at her and said nothing. *No,* he wanted to say. *Enlighten me.*

It wasn't because of all those other cases he won. It wasn't because of his golf swing, either. It was to avoid a lawsuit. They never liked him. You can say what you want, but I transcribed the minutes of all those meetings. God, I hope this isn't too much of a surprise to you.

No, he said. It isn't. Though it had never occurred to him to think about it one way or the other. Partners were partners; how they had gotten there was irrelevant.

I'm sure they've shown you the graphs, she said. But they

probably haven't told you that Jim Phillips in Brussels has been doing half the business he did last year, and no one's planning to fire him, are they? This is a setup, Marcel. They're sending you to cover their tracks.

His heart thumped, as if someone had stepped on his chest. *Should I listen to this?* Suppose that were true, he said. What would you want me to do about it?

You're a lawyer. Isn't that your job?

I am a lawyer, he said, his face getting hot. And I should warn you against making libelous statements you can't prove.

She gave a long, exaggerated sigh. Wallace is my *friend*, she said. I talk to him on the phone every week. Yes, he has some strange ideas. He's a free thinker. And he's made some questionable choices. But who hasn't, may I ask? I've known him for twenty-one years. He's the best lawyer this firm has. She put her hand on the doorknob, and twisted it, with the door still shut. Do something about it, she said. Don't pretend you don't know how.

Following the map, Marcel takes Kennedy Road to where it intersects with Queen's, along the waterfront; he crosses the road and leans against the railing, taking a breath of sea air. The water is the color and texture of ink; in the jagged reflections of a thousand lights, it seems to boil, and congeal, and dissolve again.

He remembers when his family used to go for walks in Greenwood Park, along the Hudson, and he would climb up onto the concrete barriers and lean over to stare into the water. It always smelled faintly of gasoline, a few milk containers and Coke cans bobbing up against the wall. What would happen if I fell in? he would always wonder, imagining himself thrashing in the oily muck, unable to find a handhold; and just at that moment he would feel his father's rough fingers, the fingers of a moving-company man, on the back of his collar. *Gon get yourself killed,* Marcel remembers his father saying, lifting him gently into the air and placing him back on the sidewalk. There was the reassurance, the comfort, of having those hands to catch him; but he remembers the grain of disappointment he always felt under his tongue, knowing that the danger was only imaginary, that it was a question he would never have to answer.

Wallace Ford's house is not on Hong Kong Island, as Marcel always assumed. It is on another island, with the strange name of Lamma, a mile or so to the south, and a ferry ride of forty-five minutes from Central. *We'll expect you around seven,* Ford told him. *That way you'll be on the boat while it's still daylight. It's something to see.* He sits on a plastic chair on the upper deck, facing forward, eating saltines and watching the horizon. Even looking at boats makes him a little queasy; he always remembers being sick, at four, the one time he took the Staten Island Ferry to see the Statue of Liberty. His roommate at Williams, who was on the sailing team, taught him a simple cure: soda crackers to settle the stomach, and keeping your eyes on the horizon, tricking your inner ear into thinking you're standing still. But you can hardly expect it to work here, he thinks, inhaling the smell of instant noodles and Happy Meals blowing up from the lower deck, with a folder of documents in your bag that spells the end of a man's career. The deck tilts slightly, and he grips the arms of the chair, staring fixedly at the dim silhouettes of mountains in the distance.

Excuse me?

He turns and sees a young girl sitting in the chair next to him, and beyond her, a tiny old man, holding a cane across his lap. Sorry, she says haltingly. My grandfather says you must have some sea illness. Is it true?

He nods, not knowing what to do.

He says the best thing is to sleep, the girl says. Not stay out here. There are too much noises and bad smells. She stands up, and the old man stands, too, and beckons to him, pointing at the door. For a moment he stays where he is, wanting to say, No, I'm all right. But how would she translate this; what would the old man think of his courtesy? He stands up, shakily, and follows them inside. The upstairs cabin is nearly empty, perhaps a little quieter. There, the girl says, pointing to a long row of seats. You can rest there.

All right, he says, and sits down, just to get them to leave. But they linger, watching him, and so he has to lift his legs and stretch out his long frame, his feet sticking out over the edge. *Wah,* the old man says. *Hou cheung ah!* Good, he thinks, I'm learning Chinese now. He closes his eyes, and hears the door creak and slam shut. Hell, he thinks, as long as I'm here, why not? He puts his hands behind his head and takes a deep breath.

This wasn't my choice, he repeats to himself, imagining Ford's face, those enormous, red-rimmed eyes. *I'm delivering a message. I'm sorry I have to be the one.* And then, in the moment before he falls asleep, his father's face appears in front of him. They are standing at the bus station, the day he left for Williams, waiting to load his duffel bag and new suitcase into the luggage compartment, and suddenly his father turns to him, his mouth twitching, as if to say, *don't do anything I'd be ashamed of,* or words to that effect. But the words never come. After a moment, his father looks away, picks up the enormous duffel with one hand, as if it were a paper bag, and tosses it across the sidewalk into the bus driver's hands.

He wakes when the throbbing of the engine stops, and hears feet thumping on the deck below, voices calling from the pier. The old man and the girl are gone. He stands up stiffly and sees a concrete jetty, and the low white buildings of a small village stretching along the edge of a long, curving bay.

When he steps off the gangplank, he hears someone calling his name in a high voice. Mr. Thomas? Mr. Thomas? A tall, dark-skinned woman, in a white blouse and turquoise skirt, carrying a basket of vegetables under her arm. I am Vinh, she says. I work for Mr. Ford. May I carry your bag?

No thanks, he says. I'll carry it. There's something about her face he can't quite grasp. She has high cheekbones and a long, tapering chin, and her eyes are oval: perhaps Thai, or Filipino? Or Indian? She turns, flinging a long black braid over her shoulder, and he has to hurry to keep up with her pace. They pass a row of seafood restaurants with open terraces, and stores with their wares stacked on the sidewalk: plastic tubs, straw hats, brooms, crates of oil and oyster sauce. Vinh turns left, and they climb up a sloping street, narrowly avoiding a cluster of children running at full tilt, their flip-flops slapping the ground.

Is the house far from here? Marcel asks. He never imagined Ford living in any place like this: so remote, so—*Third World,* he thinks. For lack of a better word.

A little farther, she says, waving a hand in front of them. The alley widens and levels out; now the houses are set back from the road, and spread farther apart. Here, Vinh says, and stops in front of an old iron gate spotted with flakes of red paint.

When Marcel steps inside he lets out a low whistle under his breath. The house is surrounded by an elaborate tropical garden: massive ferns, dwarf palm trees, hibiscus, oleander, birds of paradise, orchids, flowers he can't name. Ford stands on a stone pathway leading to the front door, holding a watering can, in loose cotton pants and a collarless tunic, barefoot, and Marcel suddenly is aware of the thickness of his oxford-cloth shirt, his feet sweating in tasseled loafers. The door closes, and he realizes that Vinh has disappeared into the house without a word.

Thought it would be you, Ford says, extending his hand. Excuse the informality.

Quite a place you've got here.

Oh, it's Vinh, Ford says. I just do what she tells me. A garden, you know, is a work of art. Like a painting. You can only have one painter.

My mother is just the same way, Marcel says with a tentative laugh. Ford opens the door and gestures for him to enter. Only with her it's daffodils and rhododendrons, he says, stepping inside. Not the same, I guess.

No, Ford says. Not exactly the same.

The roof of the house is a glass atrium, with windows tilted open along the sides. They sit at the end of a long dining table, underneath the branches of an enormous potted palm, and immediately Vinh begins bringing out food, dish after dish, each time scooping up the empty plates and disappearing before Marcel can thank her. He's never seen anything like it: spring rolls with black mushroom filling, rice baked in halves of a melon, a whole carp steamed in coconut milk. Ford serves them both, and eats without speaking; between courses he folds his hands on the table and breathes in deeply, staring out the window. All the better, Marcel thinks. The chopsticks are black lacquerware, with pointed ends, as slippery as knitting needles. When Ford isn't looking he shovels fish onto them with his fingers, trying not to stab himself on the tiny bones.

I'll be the first to tell you I didn't want this job, Ford says finally, leaning back in his chair, after they've finished the last course. I never was much for the international side of the business. Didn't think it was in the firm's interest to be here in the first place. But it came up just after my divorce, in 1995, and I wanted out of San Francisco. So I thought it was just the luck of the draw. And it was.

You seem to like it here.

Hell, Ford says. I'll tell you something. This position is supposed to rotate two years from now. But I'm going to ask them to make me permanent. I'll even take a lesser share if they want.

A salty taste rises in Marcel's throat. I would have thought that you'd want to go back, he says. Five years is a long time.

Ford gives him a slow, appraising look, and for the first time Marcel notices the puffiness around his eyes, the pouches at the corners of his mouth. Not so long, he says. Not when you're my age. I feel like I'm just getting started.

Marcel nods, wondering if he's supposed to understand what that means.

Peabody Stein needs a new strategy for Asia. Ford tears off part of his napkin and divides it into little squares, scattering them around the tablecloth. There is a faint buzz of anger in his voice: like a wasp trapped by a window. Right now we're operating on an outpost model, he says. We go wherever our American clients go. But the thing is, for every American company looking for a market in Asia there are three Asian companies that want a toehold in the U.S. You've got lots of young executives here that were educated at Harvard and MIT. They speak English just like we do, they eat pizza, they watch the Bulls on satellite. The problem is that we're not going after that market. The only people we're interested in are the Americans who think that the rest of the world is waiting to buy what they have to sell.

A breeze rises through the windows, smelling of oyster shells and seaweed.

But that's our primary client base, Marcel says. We'd have to do that without alienating them, right? That wouldn't be easy.

You know what I like about Hong Kong? Ford says. People here are smart. You see the stock indexes and the exchange rates right on the front page of the newspaper. He brushes the napkin fragments into his palm, and lets them fall over an empty dish, like tiny snowflakes. They aren't hypocrites the way we Americans are. They understand that money is like water: it flows everywhere, but it never changes. Doesn't matter what language it's in, or what country it comes from. If you can trade it, sell it, or exchange it, it's all the same. That's why they call it *liquid* assets, right?

Marcel presses his lips together to stifle an answer: *Aren't you forgetting the regulators? We're still members of the bar, right?* Hold on, he thinks. Why is he making this easy for me?

But enough about that, Ford says. Tell me about you, Marcel. How's the firm working out? Are you happy?

He forces himself to smile. It's hard to say, he says. Sometimes I wonder where the last five years have gone. This is my first time off in I don't know when. I didn't take a week off all last summer. Working on the Geosynch bankruptcy. Thirty thousand pages of depositions.

I heard about that. They said you guys were logging all kinds of hours.

Sure, he says. The biggest severance payment in California history. Full entailment.

I remember what it was like, Ford says. Eighty, ninety hours a week. It's a heavy price you pay. I don't think Sheryl ever forgave me for it. All those years when she would keep the dinner for me in the oven and then I would come home and fall asleep before I could eat it.

That isn't the right metaphor, Marcel thinks. A price is fixed; you know what to aim for, you know when you're finished. This kind of work is just the opposite. The question is, will you give this much, and then more, more than you ever knew you had?

I don't regret it, though, Ford says. And you won't, either.

Marcel pours himself a cup of tea, drinks it in one gulp, and gets up from the table without a word. His briefcase lies on a chair at the far end of the room; he takes the folder out and carries it back to the table in two long strides. In his hands it feels like a single sheet of onionskin, as if it might slip out of his grasp and drift away.

I'm supposed to say something before I give you this, he says. Ford stares at him impassively, his hands resting on the tabletop. I'm supposed to apologize. Blood is moving up his neck, seeping into his ears; he feels a rim of sweat on his upper lip. But I don't think there's anything I can say to dignify it, he says. So take it. Here.

Sit down, Ford says. He takes a pair of reading glasses from his shirt pocket and lets the folder fall open in his palm. His eyes dart across the page; he licks a finger and turns to the next, scans it, and turns again. Marcel's feet feel as if they are clamped to the floor. Ford snaps the folder shut and drops it on the table, nearly upsetting a bowl of peanut sauce. Sit down, he says again. Please. Drink some more tea. You don't look so good. Remember to breathe, now.

You knew, Marcel says. He grasps the armrests of his chair and eases himself down slowly, willing his muscles not to shake. You knew the whole time.

Ford shrugs again. I had a feeling, he says. When I saw you I knew for sure.

And you're not going to sue?

Ford gives a single sharp laugh. Would you? he says. If they were offering that kind of money?

Marcel's eyes are watering. I talked to Wanda Silver, he says. Before I left.

Wanda Silver is a great lady, Ford says. But she's a sentimentalist. She remembers when I used to come into work with an Afro. Don't you trust her, Marcel. She's stuck in a different era.

Is it true? About how you made partner?

That's ancient history. Ford twists his lips and rubs the edge of his mouth with his fingers. I was in the right place at the right time. There was a lawsuit. The government was getting involved, and they had to hire somebody. And I told them exactly what they wanted to hear. *My business is to win cases,* I said. *Not to cause trouble.*

You could clean up, Marcel says, in a dry, strangling voice. Punitive damages. It would be a huge case—It could set precedent all over the country.

Careful, Ford says, shaking his head slowly. You be careful, Marcel. They knew what I would do. This is about you. They want to test you. Make sure you're a team player.

To test me? Marcel says. What did they expect me to do? Throw the papers in the Bay and call the NAACP?

He gets up from the table and walks across the room, breathing hard, still tasting the sting of the curry on his lips. Overhead, the sky has gone black; he can see a dim streetlight on the road leading to the town, and a few wavering lights along the waterfront. Somewhere a radio is playing, a tune he recognizes, but with strange words; Chinese words, he realizes after a moment. He crosses his arms over his chest, and the nausea passes.

That's the South China Sea you're looking at, Ford says behind him. Vietnam is that way. China is up to your right. Canton. The Pearl River.

Marcel closes his eyes and nods.

As I understand it, Ford says, when the British came here, Hong Kong was the back of the back of beyond. No one here but a few fishermen. The emperor up in Peking didn't know this place existed. At first all they needed was a place to get fresh water for their ships and give their sailors a rest. So they set up a camp on the beach. No one noticed. They stopped here for a day or so and then kept going up the river to Canton. And you know what they had in those ships?

No.

Opium, Ford says. The crack cocaine of the nineteenth century. In a few years everyone in south China was smoking it, and the British were making so much that the Chinese were running out of money. Literally. Not enough silver to pay the bills up in Shanghai. By the time the emperor started looking at a map, the British had their warships sitting in Hong Kong Harbor and there wasn't anything he could do.

I'm not following you, Marcel says.

You're smart, Marcel, Ford says. All those East Coast schools. But sometimes I think you don't have enough dirt under your fingernails. When I was your age we were paying off witnesses at the Pacific Gas fire down in Orange County. We were giving briefcases of cash to burned men in hospital beds. Should I go on?

Don't, Marcel says. His hands are trembling; he thrusts them into his pockets. For God's sake. Enough.

We want power, Ford says. Isn't that right? We want a seat at the table. But nobody is innocent, Marcel. We're the last people on earth who can afford not to know that. Take my advice. Don't make waves. Listen carefully—and let them *know* you're listening. Someday your silence will be worth so much they'll bankrupt themselves trying to pay you off.

He stands up and holds out his hand.

Tomorrow I want you to meet me down at Exchange Square, he says. There's some friends I want to introduce you to. Business partners. You'd be amazed at the opportunities that come your way in a place like this.

When they step outside the gate Vinh lights a kerosene lantern, which crackles and sparks and gives off a whiff of greasy smoke.

You watch your step, she says. Sometimes there are snakes in the road. Be careful. Follow close behind.

I will, he says. There are insects singing all around them, unfamiliar clicks and chirps, and a low hum that reminds him of crickets, the sound of late summer evenings in Yonkers. He feels a strange sense of clearness, of spaciousness; the sensations of the world are almost unbearably vivid. The white glow of the lantern wick. The distant buzz of a motor scooter. The faint smell of incense. A small girl's voice, shouting something he can't understand.

Do you know Mr. Ford for a long time? Vinh's voice comes out of the darkness.

Not really. I met him five years ago.

You are maybe a little afraid of him.

He speeds his pace, until he is walking alongside her. Of course I am, a little, he says. He has a lot of power. He's very important. But why do you say that?

She turns her head and looks at him earnestly, her eyebrows drawn together. There is no need to be afraid, she says. He is a good man.

Sure he is, Marcel is about to say, but the words stick in his throat, and he only nods.

When I met him I did not speak English at all. Three years ago. He gives me tapes and books. Every day we have lessons. He is a good teacher.

And you are a good student. Your English is excellent.

Also he teaches me the Internet, she says. Online investments. Already I have made a little money. A pair of large moths dance around the lantern, and she brushes them away. I think the black Americans must be very generous, she says. Hong Kong people are not like this.

Marcel laughs softly. Not all black Americans, he says. We're all different. Mr. Ford is—well, Mr. Ford is special.

She nods, as if considering this idea carefully.

Vinh, he says, you're not from Hong Kong, are you? How did you come here?

From Cambodia, she says. A wisp of hair has come loose from her braid; she pushes it away from her forehead. I was a refugee. I live in the camps for a long time.

And your family?

She looks over his shoulder with a distracted smile. My parents are dead, she says. A long time ago. During the war. I have two sisters in Siem Reap.

They reach the bottom of the hill and pass along the waterfront; the seafood restaurants are crowded with families, shouting conversations across enormous round tables. The ferry has already pulled up at the pier. I should hurry, Marcel says to her. Won't it leave soon?

Wait. She brushes his arm with her fingertips, and they stop, facing one another, in the middle of the street. Her eyes are open wide, her chest rising and falling. In America he did something, she says. Yes? In America he is a criminal.

No, he says. Who told you that?

I am not stupid, she says. Tears emerge from the corners of her eyes. You tell me the truth. Mr. Ford says to me, one day we can go to America. I think he is lying. Look at your face! In America he is not free.

Marcel looks over her shoulder at the ferry. Vinh, he says, he isn't lying to you.

She takes a deep breath, and folds her arms across her chest, pursing her lips.

So what do you do now? she asks.

I don't know, he says. I need to go home. As soon as I can.

Back to San Francisco?

Yes, he says. He thinks of his apartment, his view of the city from Pacific Heights: the enormous TV covered with a layer of dust, the kitchen with three plates and two forks, the piles of dry-cleaning bags and takeout menus. An ache begins in his chest and spreads to his fingertips. I can explain all this, he thinks. I had good reasons. *I'm* not a criminal. But the words echo and fade, as if he had shouted in an empty room.

This time he falls asleep sitting up, in the same plastic seat on the forward deck, balancing his empty briefcase on his knees. He dreams that he is at a college party in Williamstown, wandering down a dark hallway lit by flickering candles, with a plastic cup of beer in his hand. He opens a door, looking for the bathroom, and walks out into Candlestick Park, the wind whipping his jacket behind him like a cape. Sheets of paper are falling from the sky, drifting, swirling, like giant snowflakes, piling in drifts around the lampposts and in the gutters. He stoops and picks one up. It is a memo, or a letter, with an address printed across the top, but the words are blurred, shifting; he brings it closer to his eyes, and sees that it is written in a strange alphabet, full of slashes and curlicues. *I need to call the office*, he says. *I need to find a translator.* He gropes in his jacket for his cell phone, but it has disappeared. All his pockets are empty. He feels water trickling around his ears, down his forehead, and starts awake, opening his eyes in a panic.

It is raining. His shirt clings to his skin, and raindrops are running down his forehead and into his eyes. He stands up; his shoes are full of water, as heavy as bricks. The ferry lurches forward under full power, the engine vibrating loudly, and through the rain he can see the shimmering lights of the skyscrapers, growing larger every second. *Get inside,* he says to himself, *you'll ruin your shirt, those are Ferragamo shoes; are you crazy?* But his feet stay rooted in place, unable, unwilling to move. The rain falling on his face is the warmest he's ever felt, warmer than rain on a hot summer day in Yonkers. He tilts his head back and sticks his tongue out: it has a slightly salty, briny taste.

I could head south, he thinks. Toward the equator. Someplace where it's eighty degrees and sunny every day, where there's no TV. No basketball. He imagines himself at the ticket counter, handing over his American Express card. *The first plane to Micronesia. To Malaysia. To Tahiti.* If I stepped onto this ferry, and then disappeared, he wonders, would they look for me? Would they even be surprised? The boat heels sideways, and he moves away from the tilt, instinctively, reaching for the rail. The city has become a wall of light, streaking, bleeding into the churning water. He grips the rail with both hands, forcing himself to stare straight ahead, until he feels the brightness surrounding him, dissolving him, as if he's stepped inside the sun. *What a relief,* he thinks, *what a relief, to be invisible.*

Revolutions

Merit and demerit are ever interpenetrated,
like light and darkness.

—Bodhidharma

In his sleep he hears the morning sounds of Chiang Mai: motorbikes and tuk-tuks whining past Tha Pae Gate, fruit sellers cursing scavenger dogs, monks' feet scuffling in the alley as they pass, collecting alms. He stirs and turns his face to the window, and even before his eyes open he knows the difference. In the kitchen the air conditioner switches itself off with a hollow rattle. He pushes himself upright and stares out at the day. Fog chokes the harbor, and the world is a study in shifting grays: pewter, charcoal, newsprint. The nearest tower blocks are faint shadows. *Hong Kong,* he tells himself, and an ache spreads through his chest, as if he's swallowed ice water. Again he wonders how it is possible, to wake in a vacuum, in the absence of sound.

In the late morning he gives himself a sponge bath and sits at the table next to the window, resting his leg brace on a chair. His sketchbook lies open in front of him, charcoal and pencils to one side. The fog has lifted, and the view is immense: the green humps of the mountains and the endless spread of Kowloon beneath them; planes landing in slow motion and traveling the length of the peninsula before slowing to a crawl; giant container ships sliding silently around the point at Kennedy Town. But the blinds might as well be drawn. He shuts his eyes and wishes for waking dreams. It has been a month and a half since he fell off a motorcycle on Surawong Road in Bangkok, and six months to a year before he will be healed and able to return to Thailand. He presses his hands over his face to shut out the light.

At two he takes the elevator to the street and hails a taxi to drive him east on Hollywood Road, stopping at a building that rises like a mirrored stele out of the antique district. *The Wong Hun Fat Rehabilitation Centre,* the sign on the office door says. For two hours he lies on a cool floor while a Buddhist nun lifts his leg slowly, a little farther each time, bending the knee so slightly that he is hardly aware of the movement. He breathes deeply, as instructed, and holds his hands cupped together below the navel. His eyes close, and he is surrounded by color fields, blue passing into violet passing into lavender. Sunlight patterns his eyelids; he tastes leaf-mold in the air. The movement that he hasn't noticed stops. He lifts his head and sees white light patterning a white floor, a gray-robed woman calling him, saying *finished, finished.*

Her name is Ji Shan Sunim. She is Polish, ordained at a Zen center in Krakow, and came to Hong Kong at the request of a teacher whose name Curtis never quite catches, a slurring of syllables that might be Hindi or Japanese. She lives in a nun's dormitory in North Point, and takes the number 87 bus to the center every day. After each session she allows him one question before rising to greet the old woman who follows him. She kneels, her hands in her lap; in the light from the window her scalp gleams like wet porcelain.

You must get tired, he says. Shouldn't you have a longer break? You'll hurt your hands.

They are not tired now.

Not today, maybe. But they will be.

The body is like a car, she says. Someday a car will break down, yes? But you don't stop driving it.

Si fu. The old woman's walker clacks on the tiles. *Si fu, leih haih bin dou ah?*

Excuse me, she says.

It seems to him there is a tiny hesitation before she stands, as if part of her wants to linger. He wishes she would. Each day, as his body loosens, his eyeballs throbbing in the heat of that imaginary sun, the willingness to paint spreads over him, and exactly at that moment she stops and draws away. His eyes open, his body cools, and he silently forgives her again. *How do you know?* he wants to ask her. As they speak her eyes never leave the floor.

After his session he crosses Hollywood Road and sits in the window of a noodle shop, drinking tea and scanning the river of passing faces, as if there's someone in Hong Kong he might recognize. Every face he sees seems fixed in dread; even the young mothers with babies seem anxious, awaiting disaster. His sketchpad sits undisturbed in the bottom of his bag.

Outside the center, the nuns wait for the bus in groups, calling out to each other and laughing loudly. They drink tea from glass jars, peel oranges and candy wrappers; a few make calls on mobile phones. When Ji Shan emerges she passes among them like a ghost and stands alone on the corner, fingering her coins; the sea winds blowing along the street flap the hems of her robe like luffing sails.

In the evening his windows are filled with the lights of Kowloon: a shimmering crescent on the black waters of the harbor, a multicolored galaxy, fascinating and unreal. He cooks with his right hip propped against the kitchen counter, stirring a pot of noodles with chopsticks, washing a handful of choi sum under the tap with the other hand. The woman who lent him the apartment has left a cabinet full of Thai spices in bottles and jars, neatly arranged and labeled in Chinese; so to replicate the recipes he learned at the cooking school in Chiang Mai he must remember the ingredients by smell: galangal and lemongrass, holy basil, oyster sauce and fish sauce. Each dish brings back a specific place. Morning in Pai, drinking tea in the street, looking west toward the mountains of the Burmese border. Bicycling through the markets above Banglamphu in Bangkok. He eats with wild anticipation, sometimes closing his eyes to focus on the scene, but even the smell dissipates too quickly, sucked away by the air-conditioning. An apartment gate clangs shut; children's feet clatter in the hall. In the silence he feels welded to his chair.

Later, lying in bed, trying to read, his eyes keep straying to the clock, remembering what time it is in America. Nine o'clock in the morning in New York; six in Santa Cruz; seven in Boulder. His friends are pouring coffee and flattening newspapers, mixing paint, switching on computers. In August he sent postcards, giving his new address, saying *I'll let you know what happens,* but since then he hasn't spoken to anyone. What would I tell them, he thinks, what is there to say?

And where are you living now?

A woman I met in Mae Hong Son loaned me her apartment. She's in France all winter, through the spring shows. She designs sunglasses. She thinks she's patronizing a famous artist.

What is Hong Kong like?

The streets are as narrow as slot canyons. Skyscrapers next to buildings that look like they've been rotting away for fifty years. Garbage haulers with mobile phones. Outside it's a sauna; inside it's always winter. Shouting is the normal mode of conversation—even in elevators.

It must be very exciting.

Colorless, compared to Chiang Mai.

Speaking of which—

I'm not working. I can't.

You have to do something. Don't you?

I still have the show in New York. That should bring in something. I don't have to pay rent; I don't need much to live on.

But you can't just stop.

Who says, he asks the ceiling. Who says what I can and can't do?

Sunim, he says, do you like living here?

In the hallway the elevator dings and the old woman screams her thanks to the attendant. The nun stares at the floor, a marble statue.

My like and dislike are not important, she says.

Why?

I am a nun, she says, raising her chin and giving him a faint smile. I do not choose. So I am free to go anywhere.

But you must get lonely sometimes.

Si fu, m'geidak—

On her knees she turns to the old woman in the doorway and bows, speaking rapidly in Chinese. The woman retreats into the hallway.

I'm sorry, he says, when she turns back to him. I shouldn't say these things. I don't know anything about Buddhism.

Do you have the same pain as before?

Sure, but I hardly notice it. I'm used to it by now.

There is a reason for this, she says. What we call pain is not really pain. It is the *fear* of pain. If you are not afraid, you still have pain, but you do not suffer.

She looks so earnest that he can't stop himself from smiling.

Let me show you something, she says. Look at this wall. Can you describe it?

It's empty, he says. Blank. Nothing on it. Just a wall.

Yes. When you expect there to be something, then there is nothing.

How else can you see it?

The wall is white. The floor is yellow.

He laughs, resting his head on the floor. I give up, he says. You win.

So feelings are also like this, she says. Always changing, coming and going. Insubstantial.

I'm taking up the old woman's time, he says. I should go.

Kneeling at his side, she drapes his arm over her neck, fits her shoulder into his armpit, and hoists him upright in a single motion. Their bodies touch for the blink of an eye; then she is walking to the door and opening it, calling *Wu tai tai, deui m'jue, deui m'jue, cheng lai la.*

We are like mirrors, she tells him, standing in the doorway.

You see me and you think she is unhappy. That is a reflection of your own fear. You see yourself in me, but you don't understand my mind.

Is that so, he starts to say, but stops himself. Sarcasm won't mean anything to her, he thinks. Her English is too literal. Then tell me, he says, what do *you* see?

The kneecap is broken, she says. The tendons were cut in many places. Now we must do stretching and massage, so the muscles do not become weak. When the bone has healed we will begin to exercise.

Is that all?

The old woman shuffles between them, banging her cane against the floor.

I am sorry, she says. Is there something else?

Her face is utterly open, attentive—expressionless, he thinks, but not in a bad way, not numb, or angry, or blank. She hardly blinks at all. It unnerves him.

No, he says. I guess not.

That night after washing the dishes he lowers himself onto the couch, propping his legs in front of him on a low stool. His stomach rumbles, his lips burning from the peppers. He folds his hands into the oval shape, closes his eyes, and tries to imagine nothing: to not imagine. For a moment he feels a sensation of weightlessness, as if he's risen an inch into the air. His nose begins to itch; he strains to keep himself from scratching it. Downstairs a door buzzes. In a distant corner of his mind he hears an old advertising jingle playing on an out-of-tune piano: *I'd like to buy the world a Coke—*He tries to slow his breathing, as she instructed, counting to seven with every exhalation, but after a few repetitions he forgets to count and has to start again. Finally he gives up and raises himself to get a drink of water. *Insubstantial,* he thinks, standing with his glass by the sink. Airplane lights blinking as a jet rises from the runway, banking, turning east.

The colors shift from blue and violet to scarlet, saffron, gold: he has passed from the forest into a meadow. His face flushes in the baking heat; dry grass crackles underfoot. Locusts are singing in trees nearby. He wants to spin around in circles, to lie down in the grass and drink the air. His heel touches something cold, and he winces; he tries to draw it away, but it is stuck there, as if to a block of ice. He shudders and gasps, opening his eyes, and looking down: his feet are resting on the floor.

Did I hurt you? she asks.

No—no. He raises his head. Outside it is almost dark, and the light in the hallway has been turned off. He can barely see her face in the gloom. What time is it? he asks.

Mrs. Wu canceled her appointment, she says. I went an extra half hour. Are you all right? Do you need some water?

It's OK, he says. It's no problem. He tries to breathe out the anger, but it remains, a fist wrapped around his windpipe.

She touches his ankle.

You are unhappy.

I am. I can't do my work here.

What work do you have?

I'm a painter. Or—I *was* a painter.

Ah.

You'll think me very self-pitying, he says. It isn't as if I'm feeding the hungry or saving sick babies. But I've been living in Thailand the last year and a half, and I've never worked so much in my life. For a while I was finishing a painting every week. And now—being here—it's all changed.

I am sorry for you.

How can you be? *Stop it,* he tells himself, *it isn't her fault, she can't control it any more than you can,* but irritation overwhelms him; her calm seems condescending, even insulting. Everything is emptiness, right? he says. Suffering isn't real. Then why should you care?

She shakes her head once, vigorously. You misunderstand, she says. It is real to you. *You* feel it.

You're goddamned right. His eyes are suddenly wet; he stares up at the ceiling, and blinks, furiously. I think it's over, he says. I don't know if I can ever get back to it.

Then there is something else you must do, she says. It could be a message. Perhaps you are not a painter at all.

He feels a sharp pain in his solar plexus; for a moment he struggles to breathe. That's easy for you to say. I've never done anything else. This is my whole life you're talking about.

Then what do you want to do?

I want to go back. I have to start over again.

She looks back at the floor. If you let go of it, she says, if you don't make here and there—if you stop always thinking *Thailand* and *Hong Kong*—it will be easier for you.

That's impossible, he says, his head rising from the floor. I don't want to play these word games anymore. How does the world exist, if you don't have *here* and *there*? I'm not a nun. I have to *choose.*

Yes, she says, giving him a defiant look. You should choose.

❖

When he says his name into the phone it echoes loudly, drowning out the receptionist's voice in New York. A long silence, and she asks again, annoyed, Curtis *who?*

Curtis Matthews for Alex Field. He represents me. The sentence repeats twice and dies away. It's a bad connection, he says. Can you hear me?

Where the hell are you?

Hong Kong, he says. Alex, it's good to hear your voice.

I'm glad you called. How's the leg?

Goddamned travel insurance wouldn't cover any of the hospitals in Bangkok. I had to leave; there wasn't any other way. This woman I met, Mrs. Mei—

He stops. Something—a tiny click, a muffled sound on the other end of the line, as if a hand has been placed over the receiver—tells him Alex isn't listening.

It's a long story, he says. I won't bother you with the details.

But you're recovering, right? That's the most important thing.

I hope I am, he says. It's hard to tell. Did you get the last paintings I sent?

We did.

And?

For a moment he wonders if the connection is broken, but he can hear the faint ticking, ticking of the timer, his Hong Kong dollars falling into space.

I think they're wonderful, Alex says. But the market's changed, Curtis. We haven't gotten the kind of interest I hoped we would. It's all swinging back to conceptualism now—nobody's looking for color anymore. Nobody cares if you can draw. You'd be amazed at the crap I've seen this season. Every figurist painter I know is having a terrible year.

He looks down and sees a sampan bobbing across the water, and for a moment he imagines it exploding, raining bits of debris on the black waves. I had a feeling, he says, willing his voice not to shake. Well, then. This is costing a fortune.

You should come back to the States, Alex says. We miss you. Everybody here misses you. You should apply for a summer residency, maybe a teaching job for the fall. Once you've recovered, I mean. Things will pick up again.

I think I may go to Mexico, he says. I've lost my taste for mescal, you know? I think I'm ready to eat the worm.

Alex gives an audible sigh, almost a groan, at the other end of the line. Don't do this, he says. It's melodramatic. It's self-pitying. It's not *like* you, Curtis. I'm saying this as your friend, understand?

Write me a letter sometime, Curtis says. Say hello to Helen, would you? He presses down the receiver and covers his face with his hands.

He wakes at the first graying of dawn, tears starting in the corners of his eyes. Images float out of his last dream. The tiny white eye of the moon above Doi Suthep. An emaciated Burmese boy curled up in the darkness of a kitchen hut, his face lit by the glowing opium in his pipe. *Now you wish you had smoked it when you had the chance,* he thinks. *Even your memories are nothing.* He turns his face to the wall, closing his eyes, but the faintest sounds invade his sleep; buses whooshing around the curve toward Central, garbage collectors calling out to one another in a hoarse singsong.

For three days he stays in bed, rising only to drag himself to the toilet. His knee is fused solid; there is no pain, but when he tries to bend it it feels as if it will snap and fall away, like a rotted branch. Clouds move fleeting shadows across the ceiling. He selects a book from the stack beside his bed, reads a few sentences at random, and lets it fall to the floor.

On the afternoon of the third day the telephone rings. He waits for the answering machine to pick up, and then remembers that there is none: in Hong Kong, where everyone has a mobile phone, there is no need. Still he feels no need to get up. Everyone who Mrs. Mei wants to speak to will know she is in Paris. But the rings persist: twenty, twenty-five, thirty-five. Finally he lurches out of bed, snatching his cane, and limps across the room to the desk.

It is Ji Shan Sunim. She sounds agitated, even angry. Why have you not come to the therapy? It is *vital* that you come every day. Have you been sick?

Yes. I've been ill. I'm sorry I haven't called.

Do you need medicine? I will send someone to get it for you.

No, he says. There's no medicine.

But you are in pain, she says after a moment. I can hear it.

I'm sorry. I don't think you would understand.

What is not to understand?

Every morning I wake up and realize that my career is over, he says. How can you know what that's like? Nuns can't fail; you can't fail if you don't *want* anything. How am I supposed to tell you about it?

In the background loud voices babble, raucous laughter rises and falls.

I don't think I can keep coming to the therapy, he says. I'm sorry. I don't think I want to get well.

Then I will come to you.

I'm not worth your time, he says. Don't bother.

What will I do, he wonders. More than an hour has passed, and he is still leaning against the desk, his back to the window. The silence burns in his ears; he taps his cane against the floor just to hear the sound. For a moment he imagines pulling the old television off its shelf in the closet and plugging it in, but no, he thinks, you do that and in a moment it will be April, and you'll have wasted five months watching bad old movies and Chinese commercials. He sees himself sitting by the window with his leg propped on a chair, washed in blue light, sweat beaded on his forehead. *Choose your poison*, he thinks. The doorbell rings.

When he opens the door she uncrosses her arms and takes off the baseball cap she has been wearing, as if to help him recognize her. She is wearing blue jeans, a pink cardigan over a yellow polo shirt someone must have loaned her, her gray nun's shoes, a small leather bag in one hand. His hand holding the cane trembles, he reaches out to the door frame for support, and she slides her hands under his arms and presses herself to him until he wonders if his ribs will collapse. She is so strong that if his good knee buckles, if he throws away his cane, she will still hold him up. *What's happening?* he hears a small, petulant voice asking. *What's she doing? You're not ready*—and he bites down on his lower lip, hard, to distract himself. *When* will *I be ready?* he thinks. *What other time is there than now?*

※

When he wakes in the morning she has already taken her blankets from the sofa and begun moving the furniture, sliding the armchairs next to the wall, turning the coffee table on its side, rolling up the carpet. On an end table she has made a makeshift altar: a tiny Buddha seated on a cigar box, a spray of dried flowers, three plums on a saucer. Her movements seem stiff, even awkward, until he realizes he's never seen her body unconcealed by robes. How uncomfortable it must be, he thinks, watching from the doorway.

Have you eaten?

There were noodles in the refrigerator, she says. She picks up the rolled carpet and folds it in half, as if it were made of paper. You don't mind?

Of course not, he says. Did you like them?

For a moment she seems confused by the question, her eyes wandering over his shoulders. Less pepper next time, she says. She balances the carpet on her shoulder and walks past him to the hall closet.

Sunim, he says, what are you doing?

My name is Ana.

Ana.

She closes the closet door and steps slowly into the light, her eyes intent on his face. I am disrobed, she says. I am no longer a nun. You understand.

But I didn't ask for that, he says. I never told you—

You should rest, she says. Taking his cane, she slides one arm under his shoulder and walks with him to the couch. Soon we start the therapy, she says. Later I will cook for you. Otherwise you will never get better.

I feel guilty, he says. Why would you disrupt your whole life for me? I didn't want this to happen.

She sits on the couch next to him and takes his hand in her lap. At first it seems to hold her full attention—she kneads the palm, rolls the loose skin of the fingers, works her thumb between the knuckles—but at the same time she opens and closes her mouth, as if straining to breathe. Finally she releases the hand and looks up at him. It is not so hard to understand, she says. I can help you. And you also can help me.

Me? he says. Look at me. I'm not in much of a position to help anyone.

She blinks twice, rapidly; a tiny, almost imperceptible flinch, and turns to look toward the door.

I'm sorry, he says. You said I had to choose, didn't you? But this isn't a choice. I don't have the faintest idea what you want from me.

Nobody will be able to help you if you are so closed, she says fiercely, turning back to him. You are like an insect. All hard around the outside.

Shell, he says, trying not to smile. The word you're looking for is *shell*.

So laugh, she says. Laugh and forget. She begins to rise, but he reaches over and catches her arm, feeling a sharp spike of pain in his thigh as he does so.

I'm sorry. I'm not making fun of you.

Her arm feels terribly fragile; expecting her to pull away, he holds it lightly, tentatively. She does not move.

Let's start this over again, he says. Don't leave.

She stares at the floor, her cheeks reddening, and he thinks, *she is embarrassed by happiness.*

You see? she says. It is not so difficult. You are helping me already.

In the afternoon she boils herbs in a pot on the stove, filling the apartment with a sour, earthy smell, and covers the floor with Mrs. Mei's monogrammed towels. When he lies down she wraps the herbs in washcloths and ties them around the brace, at the ankle and the thigh. Close your eyes, she tells him, and places a damp, hot cloth across his face. He hears her footfalls across the floor, more pots clattering on the stove; the lights dim, and her fingers pull his toes forward, cupping the heel.

What is this? he asks. You've never done this before.

My grandmother taught me.

Your grandmother?

When I was a child, we had no medicine. Even aspirin we did not have.

He remembers a movie from elementary school: *Life Behind the Iron Curtain.* Gray buildings under ashen skies; streets lined with bare trees, smoke boiling from factory chimneys. How nightmarish it seems in memory: as unreal as the bogeyman, the children who got lumps of coal in their stockings.

I wish you would tell me about Poland, he says. How you became a nun.

So many questions today, she says.

I want to keep talking. I'm a little afraid of this.

Why? It hurts?

No, he says. It feels wonderful—*too* wonderful. It's a narcotic.

A what?

Like being drunk.

You are courageous, she says after a moment. Most people would want to forget.

Courage has nothing to do with it. I've had too many hang-overs in my life, that's all.

Holding his ankle with one hand, she moves the other slowly up to his calf, gently squeezing the muscle through the holes in the brace. He feels how thin his leg has become underneath its plastic frame: a mass of tendons and nerves that quivers under her touch. When he grimaces she removes her hand and returns it to his ankle. There is a new tenderness, a slow, deliberate qual-ity in the way she handles him. He reaches up and peels away the cloth from his face. His eyes widen; the room shifts more sharply into focus around her.

To leave it on is better, she says. You can relax more.

I want to watch you. I'd rather be awake.

While she makes dinner he runs hot water in the bath and washes himself, scrubbing with the sponge until steam rises from his reddened skin. He shampoos his hair and shaves for the first time in weeks, feeling for patches of stubble with his fingers after the mirror fogs over. His muscles liquefy in the heat; his jaw feels slack, and his leg tingles when he pushes the sponge through the gaps in the brace. As if his body had forgotten the possibility of being clean. Clutching his bathrobe together in the front, he opens the door in a cloud of steam. The radio is tuned to a classical station, a Chopin prelude. She sets steaming plates on the table and turns toward him. The black dress bags slightly around her hips, and binds her chest; she wobbles on Mrs. Mei's heels like a girl dressed in her mother's clothes.

After they have eaten for some time in silence the radio program changes to big band music: Glenn Miller, Tommy Dorsey, Sinatra. He taps his good foot to the beat. I would ask you to dance, he tells her, but I never learned properly. I suppose I missed my chance.

My mother was a dancer, she says. Not that kind. Ballet. When she was very young she had a teacher from Leningrad.

Did she teach you anything?

Assemblé, she says, smiling at the forgotten word. And she gave me her costumes. I sometimes would put them on and think I was in Tchaikovsky.

You're very graceful. You would have been a beautiful dancer.

She wipes her mouth and turns to the window. High cirrus clouds hang over the city like a painted ceiling, turning the harbor lavender. Her lower jaw juts forward, as if he has insulted her and she is considering the right response. What does she see, he wonders, watching her reflection in the glass. What is there for her, in this gaudy, hallucinated world.

I wanted to tell you something, she says softly. But I don't know how to say it.

What was it?

Everything changes. Everything dies. We say, *life is a cloud which appears and disappears.* Do you understand?

Ana, he says, how could I *not* understand?

So why say it, she says. What is the use? And she reaches for his hand.

She climbs astride him and arches her back, pointing her chin at the ceiling, dropping her arms behind her: as if her body is a bow being drawn. They move as if borne by waves, in slow, even spasms, until it seems to him a continuous motion, without beginning or end. There is no building tension, no need; even the blood in his veins seems to wash back and forth in a tidal rhythm. When it is over he feels only the fading of the pulse, his body coming to rest, the air chilling his soaked face. She lies on top of him, kissing him; he is so dazed he can hardly raise his arms to embrace her. Is it what you wanted, he whispers, and she says, yes, yes, I want, I want—

The next morning is sunstruck, the sky over the Kowloon hills a faded sheet of blue, and when Ana opens the windows the apartment fills with a clean, sea-smelling breeze. He sits at the kitchen table drinking tea, turning the heavy pages of an old book from Mrs. Mei's shelf: *Some Painters of the Early Qing.* There is a chapter on Bada Shanren, the painter-turned-monk, with his scribblings of blasted scenery: gnarled trees, broken boulders, ragged, fierce-eyed birds. "The Comedy of Catastrophe," the chapter is called, and it's such an apt title that he laughs out loud. What is it? she says, coming to look over his shoulder. He gives her the book, and she pages through the chapter, looking carefully at each plate before turning to the next.

He was born into a powerful family in the Ming dynasty, he explains. Then, when the Manchus invaded, nearly everyone he knew was killed. War, famine, pillage—he saw it all. He became a monk, a wandering sage. For the last thirty years of his life he never spoke to anyone.

These are very pure, she says. Like calligraphy. I like them very much.

He's kind of a hero of mine. I've looked at his paintings for years.

You paint also in this way?

No, no. I don't have the technique. It's his thinking I'm interested in.

He had a very still mind. You can see this.

He was a crotchety old bastard, he says, and laughs. Being a monk, he was immune from prosecution. One of his friends said that when he looked at those paintings he felt that Bada Shanren was poking him in the eyes. And even now they have exactly the same effect. I think that's what every artist wants, whether they admit it or not. He stops and sips his tea. I don't know how I can talk like this, he says. I don't have the right, do I? *His* world was destroyed, utterly destroyed. And yet he knew how to respond. There's no self-pity in those paintings at all.

I think you will begin painting again soon, she says.

He closes his eyes. I'm going to disappoint you, he says. I'm not Bada Shanren.

She tilts his chin upward with her hands and kisses him on the forehead.

Don't worry about me. Don't even think that I am here.

I should show you some of my work. Would you like to see it? He looks across the room at the suitcase propped up next to the apartment door; it contains his paints, a few rolled-up canvases, and boxes of slides. He hasn't opened it since leaving Bangkok.

She reaches across the table and picks up the pencil lying next to his sketchbook. Take this, she says, handing it to him. Draw a picture right now.

Of what?

Her eyes roam across the apartment. That, she says, indicating the window.

What, Hong Kong? No, I don't do cities. No landscapes.

Not the city, then. Paint the sky.

In the mornings she works on his leg for hours, kneading the muscles of the ankle and thigh, until his back begins to cramp from lying so long on the floor. After lunch and a short rest he sits on a chair and holds his breath as she unbuckles the brace. The skin underneath is almost translucent, webbed with veins; the slightest breeze raises goose bumps across it. She raises the leg by the ankle until it is parallel with the floor, and they begin as they did two months before, with the tiniest possible motions, bending the knee so slowly that with his eyes closed he can hardly tell whether it has moved at all. Only now it is his effort, not hers; with each millimeter extended he imagines the tendons snapping like old rubber bands, and instinctively locks the knee straight again. Sweat stings in his eyes; his fingers grind against the rattan seat of the chair.

Breathe more deeply, she tells him. You are making good progress. Soon we can take the cane away.

I thought we weren't supposed to expect anything.

She smiles and caresses his ankle.

When the sun sinks into the haze above Stonecutters Island, throwing long shadows across the floor, they rise and go into the bedroom and make love without speaking. Afterward he sleeps, exhausted, and wakes in a dark room, smelling the dinner she has prepared. He reaches for the sketchpad sitting on the night table, and for the few minutes before she calls he draws straight lines and circles with his pencil, enjoying the feeling of holding it in his hand, the flow of the line away from the tip.

Stay with me, he says to her one evening as they finish eating.

Of course. She picks at the remaining rice on her plate, eating every grain. There is much work left to do, she says. You are not well yet.

I mean for good. He picks up his water glass and taps it against the table. We could go back to America. Have a house together. You could easily find a job, you know.

She stares at him patiently, unblinking: as if anything could be possible, or necessary. After a moment she wipes her mouth with a napkin. You want to be married, she says. To marry me.

Yes, he says. That's what I mean.

You would be a painter again. And I would earn money with therapy?

We could live in Boston. My parents have an apartment in Cambridge—we could rent it from them. I have friends there who would help us. There are many schools there. If you wanted, you could go back to college.

She stacks their plates and carries them into the kitchen, treading silently across the floor. I would like to study again, she says. Improve my English.

And then maybe someday we could go to Krakow.

She says nothing, and he wonders if he has mispronounced the name. Krakow, he repeats. Poland.

I was not born there, she says, over the sound of rushing water from the faucet. If that's what you mean. I was born in the country, on a farm. Near Poznan. Later I went to school in Krakow.

Where are your parents?

My father is dead. My mother does not see me.

What do you mean?

When I became a nun she would not accept me.

She comes back to the table, drying her hands on a dish towel.

But if you were married, he says, maybe she would reconsider. Anyway, we wouldn't *have* to go to Poland. Not if you didn't want to. We could go anywhere.

She smiles down at her hands, folding the towel and draping it over the back of a chair. As if laughing at her own compulsive neatness, or remembering a private joke. Sometime I would like to go to Chicago, she says.

Why there?

My mother's uncle lived there, she says. Always we talked about Chicago, when I was a child. She had many letters he wrote to her, before the war. Everything he described—the cars, the streetlights, all the different foods. So many strange English words. Michigan Avenue. Ferris wheel. I used to dream about what it would be like. And still I've never *been* there.

I think you would be disappointed.

Of course. She shrugs. Anytime, if you have a dream, you will be disappointed. Life is always that way. Still, if I have the chance, I would go.

So you don't believe in hope, he says, trying to keep his voice neutral, to avoid the note of desperation. It isn't any use making plans, then, is it?

She draws a long breath and lets it out, slowly, evenly. Hope always means desire, and desire brings suffering, she says. Like a wheel turning. One revolution.

Usually when we say that word we mean change, he says. A reversal. You know what I mean? Overthrowing something. He reaches across the table and covers her hand. When things are not the same as before.

Yes, she says. That is the difference.

He hears himself saying, in a clear, declarative voice, *I will never understand you. You'll never explain yourself, and yet I don't care.* Is there a better definition of love than that?

Before dawn she slips from his arms and lights a stick of incense on the windowsill. The burning tip and its reflection: like tiny red eyes staring at him in the darkness. Palms together, she bows, knees folding, and touches her forehead to the floor. He raises himself on his elbows. She sits up on her heels and begins to sing in a low voice, as if it is a lullaby.

> *Shin myo jang gu dae da ra ni*
> *Na mo ra da na da ra ya ya*
> *Na mak ar ya ba ro gi je sae ba ra ya*

What is that, he whispers, when she has finished. What does it mean?

A dharani, she says, staring straight ahead. A seal. A confirmation.

Confirming what?

Passing over, she says. Beginning and ending.

All day she keeps a distance between them: cleaning the bathroom while he eats breakfast at the table; sitting at the table as he bathes, drinking tea, gluing the handle to a coffee cup he dropped the night before. He leaves the door open and watches her. Between each movement her hands pause, as if there is a time delay; as if she has to remind herself of the task.

You're unhappy, he says late that afternoon. They have just finished the day's stretching, and are sitting at the table drinking tea. I can tell. You're thinking about the nunnery, aren't you?

I am sorry.

You don't have to be sorry, he says. Tell me what to do. Let me help you.

She stands and walks into the kitchen, looking out the window. The setting sun turns her face the color of straw. She puts her palms behind her waist and leans over backward. For the first time she seems tired.

I have an idea. His pulse throbs in his neck. Let's go out somewhere. I want to see the town.

See the—

You can borrow a dress from Mrs. Mei again, he says. Please.

No, she says. Not just for me. You will be exhausted.

I *love* you, he says, laughing. Do you know what that means?

Then they are standing by the curb on Hollywood Road: a woman in a slightly baggy cocktail dress and pink baseball cap, holding the arm of a tall man whose body seems tilted against her, who waves a cane at passing taxis as if to threaten them. When one finally pulls over she helps him maneuver into the backseat before sliding into the front, speaking sharply to the driver in Chinese.

Where are we going?

Downtown, she says. Lan Kwai Fong. Where the bars are.

How do you know?

The bodhisattva lives in the world but is not of the world, she says, turning to him, her face marbled by the passing neon signs: red draining into yellow draining into blue. All things to him are skillful means, she calls out, over the roar of the engine. The bodhisattva does not hesitate.

At the New Asia Club they sit next to a window that opens onto the street, buffeted by pounding music from the dance floor. It is a Tuesday, he realizes, and still the sidewalks are jammed: red-faced businessmen loosening their collars; Chinese teenagers with bleached hair and skateboards; shirtless garbagemen brushing past women in evening gowns. A line of red taxis descends the street at a crawl, blowing their horns, as if part of a never-ending New Year's parade. The noise is so terrific he feels he is underwater: it presses on his eyeballs, pushes the air out of his lungs.

Are you uncomfortable? he shouts into her ear. Do you want to leave?

She reaches across the table and squeezes his hand. I like it, she shouts. I have never been to a place like this.

You can take off your hat if you like.

Yes?

It's not so uncommon now. A woman with a shaved head.

I was wrong, he thinks. After she has removed the cap and tucked it into her evening bag men at other tables turn to look at her, glancing away as soon as he sees them. In the corner of his eye a line of staring faces at the bar. For a moment he feels the sweat running into the small of his back, the temptation to take her arm and hail the nearest taxi, but no, he decides. *The bodhisattva lives in the world.* Staring out at the street, she seems totally unaware; the corners of her mouth lift in a puzzled smile.

Excuse me.

A man sitting at the next table has risen and placed one hand on the back of her chair. Would you care to dance, his mouth says. He turns to Curtis. If you don't mind, sir, he shouts, with a heavy German accent. I see you are—

They look at each other across the table. Go, Curtis says. Try it.

She places her hand over his.

Don't be afraid, he says, mouthing the words.

After they have left he waits a full minute, counting the seconds by thousands, then takes up his cane and walks back toward the bar. An older couple moves away from the corner, giving him an unobstructed view of the dancers. Colored spotlights play at random over them, increasing in speed, then disappearing; for a few moments she disappears among the bobbing heads of the crowd. But she is there in the far corner, waving her hands awkwardly as if conducting an orchestra, grinning fiercely. He sits heavily on a stool and shouts an order into the ear of the bartender. On impulse he takes the sketchbook from his jacket pocket and drops it on the counter beside his sweating glass.

An upraised hand, a woman's ear, a snagged stocking, a sweat-darkened shirt, Ana's face, gold chains against a hairy chest. The images glow and fade imprecisely, like sunlight etched on the retina. He has been drawing furiously for an hour, filling pages with outlines that flow into one another like cursive script. They refuse to fix, he cannot see them whole; so he presses on to the next, unconcerned. Every few minutes he stops to shake the cramps from his drawing hand. *You're so out of practice,* a voice is telling him, *it's as if you're in high school again, drawing faces in a coffeehouse,* but he ignores it, gripping the edge of the table with his free hand, as if he might be dragged from his chair at any moment.

She emerges alone and stops in front of him. I have finished, she shouts over the din, would you like to—and then she sees the pen and the book open in front of him and stops, raising her hands, pressing the palms together, closing her mouth with her fingertips.

Now for the first time as they make love she moves around him, fluid and sly, slipping in and out of his grasp. *There,* she whispers to him, *that way.* And when they finish, all at once her head falls back as if pulled from behind and she cries out and pulls away, weeping.

Tell me what it is, he says, a cold knot of fear in his throat.

Do not worry, she whispers. She covers his face with her hand, passing her fingers over his eyes, the hollows of his cheeks, his lips, his chin. It is wonderful. You have begun again.

Only if it makes you happy, he says. It's because of you. It's *for* you.

Not only for me. For everyone.

No, he says, no, no. I'm allowed to be selfish this once. *Only* for you.

All right, she whispers.

In the morning he finds a note on the kitchen table, written in a shaky hand, on a blank page torn from his notebook.

To my friend,
Thank you for my happiness.
Ana

❖

A week later an unfamiliar voice buzzes him from downstairs. When the elevator door opens he sees it is a monk, an American, in the familiar gray robes. Myong Gok Sunim, the monk says, grinning and extending his hand like a car salesman from Michigan. Are you Curtis? I've come with a message from Ji Shan Sunim.

Yes?

How are you feeling? You've gone back to the *center*, right?

That's correct. Fine, he adds. Fine.

That's good. She is very concerned about you.

Likewise, Curtis says. I hope she has made the right decision. Funny American, he thinks, face as wide as a side of beef; feelings seem hardly to register, like tiny ripples around the edges of a pond. Then he thinks, *look in a mirror sometime.*

She wanted to let you know that she's leaving for Korea in a few days.

She'll be accepted back in?

Anyone can take refuge, the monk says. No matter what they've done. Coming and going—that's how life is, right?

Wonderful, he says, but his voice breaks in mid-syllable; Myong Gok Sunim looks at his hands. Tell her I've been painting, he says. He turns and limps back into the lobby.

Thin, she thinks, but not too thin; he's eaten the lentils I left in the refrigerator, used my sauce on his noodles. I should have written out recipes, and told him how to order the proper vegetables from the supermarket: all he knows to cook are things that will burn his insides away. She tilts her head so both eyes can see around the doorway. As he talks to Sunim he balances himself against his cane with both hands, like a picture of an old master leaning on his staff and talking to a frog. What a teacher he will be someday, to someone, she thinks. She closes her eyes. They are asleep again, his broad forearms locked around her waist, and in her dream a swallow veers above a golden wheat-field and lights on a fence post, preening in the morning sun. *There are no swallows there,* she thinks, *not in midsummer.* Tears spatter the rain-blackened pavement. She looks up to see him and he is gone.

Heaven
Lake

M y daughters are almost grown: sixteen and twelve. Mei-ling, the elder, makes her own cup of coffee, and twists her hair into a careless rope at the breakfast table; Mei-po, tall and slender as a rice shoot, carries a backpack that weighs thirty pounds, as if at any moment she could be summoned to climb Mount Everest. They move through the apartment beginning at dawn: I open my eyes to the sound of the shower running, bare heels knocking along the hallway, a burst of music, a door slammed shut. When I walk into the kitchen, their eyes slide from the table to the floor to the television without looking up. *Zao,* I say, morning, and they stiffen, as if I've dropped a glass, or scraped my nails against a chalkboard. Sometimes I imagine I've stumbled into an opera at the pause between the overture and the aria, and at any moment their voices will twine together in lament. *Our father keeps us captive in his castle,* I can hear them sing. *Rescue us!*

Of course there's nothing wrong with them. They are sensitive, untouchable things—like butterflies that have just broken their cocoons. If their mother were alive, she would say, *Let them be. Enjoy the silence.* And perhaps I should. In the six years since she left this world I've learned to make French braids and instant noodles, and memorized the names of a hundred pop singers. I imagine I am the only teacher of comparative philosophy who has ever shaken hands with the Backstreet Boys. How hard can it be, after all that, to learn to be ignored? But when I sit next to them, bent over a cup of tea and the *Ming Pao,* and no one says a word, I have a feeling I can't easily describe. It's as if my heart has puffed up inside my chest like a balloon, and every beat presses against my ribs, like the thump of a muffled drum. It's nothing, my doctor says, but he's wrong. That beat is the sound of time passing. I stare down at my newspaper and think, *No, it's not so easy. Silence is not a luxury for me.*

Look, Mei-ling tells her sister, flipping the pages of a fashion magazine. In July she will go to Paris, to finish her last year of high school at the American University there. She stabs a finger at a picture. It's where all the models live, she says. In the fifth arrondissement.

Mei-po looks curiously over her shoulder. I thought you said Monaco, she says.

That's for the *winter.* In the spring you have to be in Paris. Everyone knows that.

I raise my head. Don't get any ideas, I say. You're going there to study. Not to have men taking pictures of you.

I know that, she says. I *know.* Her eyes flicker across my face and she turns her head away. Old man, I hear her thinking, what more do you have to say to me? Tell me something I haven't heard before.

And I have an answer for her, too. That's the worst of it.

After they've left, in the pale morning light, I put on my favorite CD—Rostropovich, the Bach unaccompanied cello suites—and pace the floor in my socks, soundless. Outside my windows the March sun burns away the mist, and if I wanted to, I could look out all the way across Tolo Harbor to the eight peaks, the Eight Immortals, their broad green slopes dappled with cloud shadows. But I don't. I've lived in Hong Kong for thirteen years, and it has always seemed unreal to me, so clean and bright, like a picture postcard some clever photographer has retouched. In my study there are stacks of papers to grade, books I should have read and reviewed months ago, but I have no concentration: the time slips through my fingers like water. I whisper my daughters' names to the air and say, *Listen. Listen to me.*

When I was your age, I was just like you. I thought that everything in my life had happened by accident. I decided that when I was old enough I'd go to the other side of the world. Everyone said that it was impossible, but I worked hard, and waited, and finally my chance came. And then—

And then?

Why should it be so difficult to explain?

In the fall of 1982, when I was nineteen, I went to New York City from Wuhan, China; I had won a government competition and received a special scholarship to study at Columbia University. It's hard for me to imagine, now, how innocent I was. New York then was not like those television shows my daughters watch, where young people stroll the streets, laughing and making jokes. At that time muggings were so common that no one went outside unless they had to, even during the day. After sunset the shop owners pulled grates over their storefronts to keep robbers from breaking the windows; even in the dormitories we locked ourselves into our rooms three times over. On warm nights that September I stuck my head out my window in the International House and looked up and down Claremont Avenue, searching for a single person in the street. The buildings were as faceless as prisons. I knew New York was the biggest city in the world, that there were twelve million people hidden behind those walls, and yet I felt as if I had been locked in an isolation chamber. I thought, *Either I'll go insane in here or I'll be killed by a madman on the street. How can anyone live this way?*

The problem was that I had to make money. Even with my tuition and my books and my room paid for I didn't have enough to eat three meals a day. Though it rained all through that first October, I couldn't buy an umbrella, or new shoes to replace the ones I'd brought with me from home. I wore the same ragged suit to class every day, and the other students stared at me. I was humiliated. In China my family was not poor; my father had survived the Cultural Revolution, and had been reinstated to his post in the history department at Huizhong University. But then, of course, in China everyone wore the same clothes day after day, unless they were fabulously wealthy. There were many times that term when I looked out the windows of my classroom at the American students in their fashionable ragged shirts and jeans worn through at the knees, and wished I could go to the scholarship office and ask for a ticket back to Beijing, where at least they didn't make promises they couldn't keep.

But the answer was much closer at hand. One day on the bulletin board in the International House lobby I saw an index card of scribbled characters. *Make Money Now Without A Work Visa. Just Call Wu,* it said, and gave a telephone number.

You're a student? he asked in Chinese, as soon as he heard my voice.

I live in the International House—

Come to Fifty-sixth and Broadway, he said. Look for the Lucky Dragon.

Yes—

He slammed down the phone.

The Lucky Dragon was a Chinese restaurant on a busy corner in midtown, with enormous dark windows that reflected the street. I stood on the sidewalk for a moment, trying to comb my hair with my fingers, and then cupped my hands to the glass. I was astonished. There were no Chinese there, only Americans, whites and blacks and Latins, eating on enormous American plates, with forks and knives, drinking cocktails and Coca-Cola. The woman at the register saw me and shouted something, and an enormously fat man came out of the kitchen and opened the door. He wore a white jacket that looked as if someone had vomited on it. Speak English? he barked at me in Mandarin, with a thick Cantonese accent.

Yes.

Do sums without an abacus?

Of course.

Ride a bicycle?

I burst out laughing, despite myself. Asking a person from China whether he can ride a bicycle is like asking a fish if he can swim. Only in Hong Kong do Chinese people ride bicycles for exercise.

Good, Wu said. I'll give you a map. The bicycle is down in the basement.

Uncle, I said, what will I be doing?

Chinese food delivery! he shouted at me in English, his eyes nearly popping out of his head. Twenty minutes or less! What did you think, Mr. Peking Duck?

At first I was always afraid. I studied the map that Wu gave me until I could reproduce every cross-street in my mind, so that I'd never have to stop, never ask directions. I rode with the heavy bicycle chain looped around my shoulder, the lock undone; if someone grabbed me from behind, I told myself, I would swing it around and strike. Another delivery boy showed me how to tie a white cloth across my forehead so I would look like the *gongfu* actor Bruce Lee. If someone tries to mug you, he said, just wave your arms and make a face and shout a lot. They'll leave you alone. But really I knew I'd never have the courage to fight. I was a fast bicycle rider, and that was what I relied on. Each delivery was like a mission into enemy territory, and I returned at the edge of panic, whipping between delivery trucks and taxis, as if fox ghosts and ox demons pursued me.

For a month I worked this way, four nights a week; then I relaxed a little, and began to look around, reading the signs as I rode. Jake's Deli. The Floral Arcade. Columbus Circle. The Sherry-Netherland. In the theater district I learned the network of alleys and side streets where the stage doors were, where men in black clothes snatched the bags and thrust wads of money into my hand: sometimes twenty dollars for a fifteen-dollar order, sometimes ten for thirteen fifty. On Central Park West, the doormen waved me inside impatiently, and old women living alone lectured me on staying warm and keeping safe. I interrupted arguments, let cats escape past my ankles, and held crying babies while their mothers counted out the last penny of their order, nothing extra.

The money was terrible—I know that now. But at the time it seemed like a fortune: enough for a winter coat and a pair of boots at Woolworth's, and five shirts for fifty cents each at the Salvation Army. And when I glided into the alley behind the Lucky Dragon I felt very happy. To me it was a great adventure, the kind of thing I had never imagined in my parents' apartment in Wuhan. Who would have thought that I would move freely and alone through the streets of New York City, speaking the language, handling the money, as if I belonged there, as if it was nothing extraordinary at all?

I wish that were the end of the story. I'd give anything for that.

At eleven o'clock on a Thursday night in late October, one last order came in from Tenth Avenue. Two bags of food, so heavy the kitchen boy grunted as he carried them out the door. I looked at the receipt—three orange chicken, two moo shu pork, six egg rolls—and raised my eyebrows when I came to the bottom. Forty-three dollars. Who had that kind of money to spend on Chinese food?

They said it's a birthday party, Wu shouted at me from the doorway. He had a cleaver in one hand and a scalded chicken by the neck in the other; blood ran down the edge of the blade and dripped onto his shoes. Promised a big tip. Don't worry.

I thought we didn't deliver past Eighth Avenue at night.

If you don't want it, anyone else will take it. *Daak m'daak a?*

Daak, I said. Fine. I pushed away from the curb carelessly, balancing on one pedal, as I'd seen the other delivery boys do. But when I passed the last lit bodega at the corner of Fifty-second and Ninth, I cursed my bravado. It was a neighborhood where the warehouses and garages didn't even have windows, only blank walls and steel doors bolted shut. Most of the streetlights were broken: I sped from one small pool of light to the next, sometimes half a block away. When I turned onto Tenth I could feel the sweat pooling under my arms, on my chest, at the base of my throat. But here, at last, there was a light: a storefront, its windows covered with brown paper, glowing like a lantern at the Moon Festival. I checked the number: this was the place. There were no sounds coming from inside, but still, I was relieved. As long as the address was right—as long as no one stepped out of the shadows and brained me with a brick—the delivery was all right. By that time I had made hundreds of trips from the Lucky Dragon; perhaps I thought I was invincible.

The door opened a few inches when I knocked, and a face appeared in the crack: a nose, a thin mustache, and lips, the eyes hidden from view. Who is it?

You order Chinese food?

The face disappeared, and the door swung wide open. I took a step forward and all at once the lights switched off and two hands pushed me to the side; I dropped one of the bags and swung the other in front of me. It struck nothing, and flew from my fingers, and I heard it hit the floor with a heavy thud. The door slammed shut; I was sealed in darkness. The hands pushed me again, and my shoulders bumped against a wall. Hold still! the same voice said. I got a gun! Hold still!

OK! I said. OK! No problem! I put my hands up in the air. What you want?

Shut up for a second. A flashlight beam swept across the floor and into my face; I winced, and closed my eyes. Where's the money?

I reached under my shirt and unbuckled the belt we used to carry change. I don't see you, I said, holding it out. I don't see you, you let me go, OK?

The light dropped from my face. I heard the pouch unzipping, coins tinkling on the floor. Fuck! he hissed. Fuck! This all you got? Ten bucks?

Delivery only carry ten.

Where's your wallet?

I took it from my front pocket and held it out. I have nothing, I said. I am poor.

I heard it slap against the floor, on the other side of the room. *My wallet*, I thought. It was the first thing I had bought in America, at Krieger's Stationery on 112th and Broadway—to keep my new student ID card and a copy of my visa, a picture of my parents and my brother and sister. The room smelled of spilled Chinese food: garlic and ginger and the too-sweet orange sauce that Americans liked. If I have to die, I thought, let it be here. Don't let him take me away from my parents' faces and the smell of my own food.

I don't see you, I said, more loudly this time. I won't say anything. You let me go.

There was no answer. I opened my eyes. The flashlight was lying on the floor, throwing a dim half-moon against the front wall. He was crouched down with his back to the door: a small, pale man, hardly bigger than me, wearing an open-neck shirt and black polyester pants, holding his head in his hands. Beside him, on the ground, was a tiny silver pistol, shining like a child's toy.

You got to help me, Chinaman, he said, his voice muffled by his palms. I got ten minutes to get seventy bucks.

But I have no money.

Yeah, no shit, he said. You got friends? There's a phone in the back. You got family here? Someone with a car?

All my family in China.

You sure? He dropped his hands and looked at me: a handsome face, I thought, thin and angular, except for a long pink scar descending from the corner of his mouth. You got no cousins in Chinatown? Aren't you supposed to all be cousins? Chin, Chong, Wong, like that?

My name is Liu.

Shit. He gave a sudden, high-pitched laugh, like a small dog barking. My damn luck, he said. Me and the loneliest gook in New York.

Why you need this seventy buck?

He looked at me incredulously, as if I'd asked him why the sun went down at night. I got debts, man. Serious debts.

You don't have job? Don't make money?

Yeah, I got a job. I run the numbers. You know what that means?

I nodded, though I had no idea.

I work for Ronnie Francis, he said, as if it were a name that everyone knew, like Nixon, or Colonel Sanders. Ronnie don't mess around. Last time I took a little extra off the top, this is what he did. He held up his hand in front of him, the fingers splayed. I squinted in the half-light, and saw that his little finger was a stump, cut off at the knuckle.

This time I'm dead, he said. Ronnie promised me. I only get one warning.

I can not help you, I said in my loudest, most American voice. I am only delivery man. I don't come home, my roommate calls police.

He stared at me for a moment without speaking. Chinaman, he said, you don't get it. Time the police get here we'll both be gone.

I felt a tingling sensation rise from my toes, as if I'd just stepped into a freezing bath. *I'm his ransom,* I thought. *I'm his way out. He'll never let me go.* And then I thought, *give him something. He's desperate—he'll believe you.*

Why stay here? I asked. You hide somewhere else.

He picked up the pistol and stood, wrapping his arms around his chest and shaking from side to side, as if he were freezing cold. Can't, he said. Ronnie's got spotters everywhere. I couldn't even get a bus out of Port Authority.

I call my boss, I said. He find someone take you to New Jersey. Easy. You pay him later.

After I kidnap his delivery boy?

He don't care about me, I said. Only about money. You tell him you pay one hundred dollars, he take you anywhere.

He didn't answer, but walked to the window and peeled away a scrap of paper so that he could look out at the street.

Chinese delivery van, I said. No windows. No one see you. You want me to call?

I got a cousin in Newark, he said. His voice had grown raspy, as if something was swollen in his throat. My sister's in Philly. He looked down at the tiny gun, and out the window again. Would you do that for me?

Give me the light, I said. He tossed it over. I picked my way to the back of the room, stepping over a pile of broken bricks, batting cobwebs and loose wires from my face. The telephone was on the floor in one corner, connected to a raw copper wire. I squatted next to it, and dialed the only number I knew: the office of my department at Columbia. I covered the mouthpiece and spoke loudly in Chinese. Father, I said, using his proper name, I hope you can hear me. I am about to do a terrible thing. You must forgive me. And then I said yes a few times, *hao*, *hao*, to make it seem like an agreement, and slammed down the phone.

We walk around the corner, I said. I turned and saw my wallet lying against the wall, a few feet away; I picked it up and put it back in my pocket, my fingers trembling. Hide behind Dumpster, I said. He meet us there.

When I was a child in Wuhan, during the Cultural Revolution, the Red Guards that ruled our city split into factions and fought battles in the streets, with sticks and knives, with machine guns and hand grenades. In those years I learned many extraordinary things; one of them is that a small pistol can only be fired accurately from a few feet away. If I was able to get away from this man, and run, I was sure that he would miss. This is what was in my mind as we left the building and walked along Tenth Avenue, toward Fifty-second; as soon as we turned the corner, I thought,

I would sprint away, zigzagging from side to side, to make it harder for him to aim.

Can't believe it, he said, as we walked. He seemed even smaller than he had inside, hunched over, darting glances up and down the street. His voice was almost tearful. Once I get out, that's it, he said. Can't ever come back to the Apple. Ronnie Francis, man, even I showed up after he was dead, his ghost would track me down and get me.

I said nothing. My eyes were locked on the corner, estimating the number of steps it would take, and wondering whether I should simply run, or shove him aside first, to give myself an extra second or two.

My name's William, he said. My friends call me Willie. What's your name, man?

Liu, I said. My name is Liu.

What the hell kind of a name is that? Loo? That's a girl's name, man. Like Lucinda, or Lulu, or something. No, I got a name for you. You're from the Lucky Dragon, right? So you're Mr. Lucky. You're my luck, man.

OK. Mr. Lucky, I said, barely hearing him.

I got a bad feeling. He took a long, trembling breath, and wrapped his arms around his chest again, although it was a warm, humid night for October. I feel like I'm going to die, man, he said. I'm scared.

You not going to die, I said. Everything fine. Soon the van come.

Tell me a story, he said. Would you do that? Just to get my mind off it.

We were twenty feet from the corner now, six or seven paces, and my body was tingling, sizzling, as if I'd jammed my finger into an electric socket. I was tempted to leap on him and wrestle the gun away, although I knew that that, more than anything, could easily get me killed. I clenched my fists so hard the nails tore my skin. I don't know any stories, I said. I'm sorry.

Come on! He was breathing so hard I thought he might have a heart attack. Everybody knows a story. Gimme a break, man!

All right. I closed my eyes for a moment, and heard a string of Chinese words, out of nowhere; at first I didn't recognize them at all. There was a fish, I said. A giant fish in the northern ocean. And it changed to a bird—a bird big as the whole sky. This bird flew to the Heaven Lake.

William nodded vigorously. That's cool, he said. I like it. The Heaven Lake. So where's that? Where's Heaven Lake?

We had almost reached the corner, and the muscles in my legs were tensed to run; I felt as if I were walking on stilts. A taxi rounded the corner and sped up Tenth Avenue, and I turned to make sure it didn't stop; and that's when I saw the blue car, coming slowly down the street from the opposite direction. It was a Chevrolet, I think, and one door was painted a different color, as if it had been replaced. It was driving with its lights off. Two men were sitting in the front, and I could see their arms and chests in the glow of the streetlights, their faces hidden in shadow.

Come on, man, William said to me. Heaven Lake! Don't stop now.

The car sped up and pulled alongside us, the driver's door opening as it moved.

Hey, Willie. Where you going, Willie?

William stopped, and his mouth sagged open, like a child caught sneaking a piece of candy. He turned around, and I stepped away from him. I wanted to run, but my legs locked at the knees; instead, I folded my arms in front of my chest, as if that would protect me.

Hey, William said, his voice cracking. Curt. It's OK, man. I was just waiting for you.

Curt stepped out of the car and stared over William's shoulder at me. He was tall, dressed in a tan leather coat, and his eyes were the palest blue I'd ever seen, like a cat's eyes. I squeezed my arms tight around my chest; my ribs felt ready to crack.

This is Mr. Loo, William said. He's going to get me a little loan. I'll have it for Ronnie tomorrow. I swear.

That true?

I swallowed hard; my mouth tasted as if it were coated with dirt. I looked at Curt's face, and his hands hanging open at his sides, and I thought, *he'll know. He'll know if you're lying.* I shook my head slowly.

Get in the car, Curt said to William.

What? Why? I just said I was—

Curt grabbed William's wrist and bent his arm back, took his shirt by the collar, and swung him around, banging him against the side of the car. William turned his head and stared at me. Call the police! he shouted. Call the police! The rear door swung open, as if by magic, and Curt pushed him inside and slammed it. Then he turned to me, and took out his wallet. Charlie, he said. Hey. Charlie. Here's fifty bucks. He threw the bills in front of him, and they scattered on the sidewalk like loose napkins, bits of trash. Everything's OK, he said. Get down on the ground. Don't look up. Please. You understand me?

I understand, I said.

Then get down there. And count to a hundred.

I did what he said. I pressed my face to the sidewalk until the car rounded the corner, and then raised my head. There were no shouts, no sirens; only the echo of my own breathing. I stood up slowly, leaning forward, my hands on my knees. After a minute I broke into a run. I unlocked my bicycle and pedaled furiously away, taking a long, circling route. When I finally reached the Lucky Dragon I left the bicycle and chain at the back door.

I am a teacher of philosophy. My gods, if I have gods, are ancient, dry-lipped men, who stay awake in the small hours worrying over the substitution of one word for another. *Yi*, for example, which means righteousness. *Ren*, which means benevolence: the love of a father for his children, the love of one man for all men. I speak of these things in my seminars, and often my young students, who are the same age that I was in 1982, say, *there are no exceptions. Kant was right. Mencius was right.* I look at them and I think of myself lying in bed in the International House that night, rolling over and over, the sheet coiled around me like a rope. There was a telephone next to my bed, and a white sticker on the side that said EMERGENCY CALL 911. I could see William's face, twisted in pain, and then I thought of my father, and how the police nearly beat him to death in 1968, when he dared to report the murder of his friend. I think of these things, and I look at my students and say, *No. It's not our job to decide.*

In the *Nicomachean Ethics*, Aristotle says, *In some cases there is no praise, but there is pardon, whenever someone does a wrong action because of conditions that no one would endure.* Sometimes I take great comfort from this. Not because I feel guilty for saving my own life. No, because I know there are people who would say that William deserved to suffer, and that I was brave, like an action hero. Even my own daughters, I think, would look at me with new admiration: as if I were like Schwarzenegger, who always rolls away from the cliff, or turns so that the knife strikes the other man instead. This is why I like the word *pardon*. A pardon is a little space, an opening, where the world stands back and leaves you alone. It is the door I walk through every day when I open my eyes.

Here is my problem, again: *I* understand perfectly. But a pardon isn't an explanation; it isn't something to pass on to your children. A pardon is the opposite of a story.

The CD is finished: its fourth repetition. The sun pours through my windows, and the water of the harbor has turned a bright blue-green, the color of laundry soap. It strikes me, now, how foolish I am to think this way. Another man would be able to say, *this is what I've learned from my life*. And he would include everything I haven't: the woman named An Yi I met later that year in the International House cafeteria, and how we struggled for five years in New York while I finished my degree; how Mei-ling was born one night in the Columbia Presbyterian hospital during a driving rainstorm in June. How we came here, to Hong Kong, and how the cancer in An Yi's breast took her and left me alone with two small children and a heart as hollow as a Buddhist's wooden drum. I try to hold it all in my mind at once, and it slips away from me, like my shadow; as if I'd raised my hands to cup the light that falls across the floor.

Where is Heaven Lake?

In the ancient tale, it was the home of the Immortals; a place we humans could never reach. But this is what I think: in this world there are no more Immortals. We cross the oceans in a matter of hours; we talk to people thousands of miles away; we even visit the moon. So if Heaven Lake exists, it is wherever we are, right in front of us. Even here, in this strange city, where I so often wake up and wonder if I am still dreaming. And it may be that stories do not have to have endings we understand, any more than human lives do. Perhaps beginnings are enough.

It is four o'clock. My daughters are on their way home; standing together in a crowded subway car, rolling up the sleeves of their uniforms, loosening their Peter Pan collars. Mei-ling is listening to her Walkman, and reading a fashion magazine; Mei-po pages quickly through a Japanese comic book she's borrowed from a friend, the kind I won't let her read. If my wife were alive, I would ask her: *is this what it means to have children? To be able to see them so clearly, and never know what to say?* I am not any kind of storyteller, but my daughters are coming to my door, in these precious last days, and I have to give them something. They come in, and let their heavy bags drop with a thud that shakes the apartment, and turn to see an old man standing with his arms open, and his mouth is open, as if he is about to sing.

Notes

"Revolutions": The epigraph of this story is taken from an essay attributed to Bodhidharma, "The Twofold Entrance to the Tao," translated by John C. H. Wu in *The Golden Age of Zen*. The line from the Great Dharani *(shin-myo jang-gu dae-da-ra-ni)* is taken from the daily liturgy of the Kwan Um School of Zen.

"Heaven Lake": The story of the fish turning into a bird is taken from the first sentence of the "Free and Easy Wandering" chapter of the *Zhuangzi* (Chuang-tzu), interpreted by the author.

In writing "The American Girl," I was aided greatly by two oral histories of the Cultural Revolution: Anne Aitken's *Enemies of the People* and Feng Jicai's *Voices from the Whirlwind*. I would like to express my gratitude for their work.

Acknowledgments

This book would not have been possible without the support of the Yale-China Association and the Chinese University of Hong Kong, who made it possible for me to live and work in Hong Kong from 1997 to 1999. Zen Master Dae Kwan (formerly Ven. Hyang Um Sunim) and the sangha of the Su Bong Zen Monastery provided invaluable support during my time there, as did, in different ways, David Bailey, Caroline Ross, Brian Seibert, Yonnie Kwok, Youru Wang, Mimi Ho, and Bill and Chenghui Watkins. Many thanks, also, to Charles Baxter, Nicholas Delbanco, Peter Ho Davies, and Reginald McKnight, and to Sean Norton, Jennifer Metsker, Aaron Matz, and Melanie Conroy-Goldman. Maybelle Hsueh and Christina Thompson provided vital editorial assistance. I'm deeply grateful to Elyse Cheney, my agent, who has worked tirelessly on my behalf, and Susan Kamil, my editor, who has an uncompromising eye and a fierce dedication to literature. My parents, Constance and Clark Row, have been as generous with their support and love as any parents could possibly be. Last, my greatest thanks go to my wife and best friend, Sonya Posmentier, who believed in these stories before I did.

About the Author

Jess Row taught English at the Chinese University of Hong Kong from 1997 to 1999, the two years immediately following the handover of Hong Kong to China. His stories have appeared in *The Best American Short Stories 2001* and *2003* and *The Pushcart Prize XXVI*, and he has received a Whiting Writers' Award and a fellowship in fiction from the National Endowment for the Arts. He lives in New York City and teaches at Montclair State University.